ALPHA MOUNTAIN: REBEL

BOOK 2

VANESSA VALE

RENEE ROSE

Alpha Mountain: Rebel

Cover design: Bridger Media

Cover graphic: Deposit Photos: Fourleaflovers, appalachianview

ALPHA MOUNTAIN: REBEL
A Mountain Man Mercenary Romance

Breaking the law has never been more appealing.
She's the law in town. Holds the handcuffs.
The beautiful deputy can put them on me. *Anytime.*

One look, and I'd do anything for the woman.
Even help her break every rule she's vowed to
uphold.
Because sometimes doing things wrong is the only
way to make it right.

**Enjoy the next standalone romance from Alpha
Mountain, where a band of ex-Navy SEALs turned
mercenaries will move mountains to protect and
claim their women.**

PROLOGUE

MEGAN

I EASED the slender metal pry tool from my pocket and wedged it under the edge of the ceiling vent. A drop of sweat from my forehead hit the metal ductwork.

"Where are you, Meggie?" My dad's voice was terse in the comms unit in my ear.

"About to drop down," I murmured back, carefully pulling the vent cover beside me. My lanky, teenage body was wedged into the duct of the Tatum Auction House, twenty feet above the display case holding the Blue Empress Ring–a flawless Burmese sapphire set with baguette diamonds valued at over three million dollars. It was on display for viewing but was set to be sold Saturday. The window to nab the jewelry was now or never.

"The timeline moved up by five minutes."

I froze. *Five minutes.* "Why?"

"Calculating error in the security system reboot. Looks like it's coming online faster than expected."

"What?" I whisper-shouted. Panic shot through me. I needed that time and a miscalculation was not part of the plan.

"Keep your cool. Do your job and get out, just like we rehearsed. There's still plenty of time."

That was easy for him to say. He was sitting in a van across the street with his eyes on a computer monitor. I was the one who would be caught if things went south. I was the one who was limber and small and fit and... all things he wasn't.

But I trusted him. He knew what he was doing. We'd done this before. We were partners. Dad and daughter. A duo.

I eased the ceiling plate back, so I didn't bump it and clipped my harness to the support rod. Slowly, slowly, I lowered myself into the room, head first to start, then I flipped my feet down to rappel. The lasers were still up, but the security monitoring cams were down.

"Ready," I whispered when I hovered directly above the display case.

"Knocking out the power now." My dad's deep, reassuring voice sounded in my ear.

The lasers winked out.

I lowered myself another six inches, then clipped off to hold in place to pick the lock of the glass display case. The first time my dad and I had gone rappelling, it hadn't been in a building but down the side of a mountain in Montana. Far from here.

"Hello there, beautiful," I murmured to the Empress. She was stunning, even in the dark. Or maybe my reverence stemmed from the months of research we'd done about her.

I worked the lock of the case. It should've only taken me thirty seconds.

We'd practiced it hundreds of times.

But the angle was weird with me hanging over it instead of sitting or standing in front as I'd practiced. I couldn't quite get the feel of the pins in the lock.

"*Meg.*" My dad's voice was terse, making me jump and lose my place in the lock. "Do you have it?"

I bit my cheek, not wanting to admit my failure. "Almost," I lied.

Crap!

This was the big job–the type my dad had been

grooming me for the past three years. The little ones had all been practice. *For fun.*

I was not going to screw it up. I couldn't let him down.

I closed my eyes and took a deep breath. Let out the air and started over.

There. I finally unlocked it. I lifted the glass away and grabbed the Empress, sliding it on my middle finger. "*Got it.*"

Exhilaration shot through me as I held our prize.

"Get out of there."

I'd never heard my dad's voice so tight, but we'd never done jobs this big together before.

I unlocked the rope and clicked the button to activate the miniature winch to haul me up.

That was when all hell broke loose.

The lasers came on. The alarm blared.

All my training went out the window, and I froze, even though I rose higher and higher. Panic kicked in, nerves firing. Oh my God!

"*Dad?*"

"Meg, get out!"

Well, duh.

My head hit the support beam in the ductwork as the winch continued to raise me as I grimaced. Sweating, trembling, I crawled back in and replaced the vent cover with shaky hands, just as the interior lights flew on and shouts sounded.

Fuck.

My heart pounded.

The police were there. Or the auction house security.

It was okay. I could still get out.

"Dad?" I whisper-hissed.

He didn't answer.

"Dad!"

What in the hell had happened to him? Had he been picked up?

Okay. It was okay. We'd never once trained for the possibility that a job would be botched in some way. I didn't know what to do. I forced myself to take a breath and exhale before I moved.

I could stay in these ducts all night if I had to. No one knew I was here.

But as soon as I had the thought, I got claustrophobic. It didn't make sense–I'd never been this way before, and I had a fair amount of practice with scrabbling through ducts and other small spaces.

I army crawled through the narrow passage as fast as my forearms could carry me, praying I wasn't making too much noise. I arrived at the drop-down, a ten-foot free fall, and didn't blink before taking it.

I landed hard, and my ankle wrenched beneath me, sending a lightning bolt of pain up my leg. I didn't quite manage to keep my cry muffled, and I reached down instinctively to wrap my fingers around the spot. It was okay, though. I was almost out. Once I was on the street, I could slip into the night. Or hobble.

I went to the next set of ducts and slithered forward until I got to the end in the boiler room. From there, I only had to crawl through an upper window, and I was out.

I hoisted myself up and tossed my legs through the opening then dropped quietly to my feet, my right leg buckling a little because of the sore ankle.

"Face down, hands behind your head!"

I froze at the shouted command. Three officers had me cornered with guns pointed at me. They were big, burly, and very angry.

"I said, face down!" the guy snapped.

"Nice and easy, no fast moves," another added.

Slowly, I dropped to my knees, hands in the air.

"Where's your partner?" the first guy asked. "You couldn't have pulled this off alone, kid."

That was when I realized that they hadn't caught my dad. They didn't know where he was. Or who he was.

They hadn't caught him. Why? Because he'd run away. The comm in my ear was silent because he was gone.

As the Empress sapphire ring was taken from me and cuffs slapped on my wrists, I knew what he'd done. He'd left his seventeen-year-old daughter to take the fall for his crime.

CHAPTER ONE

Twelve Years Later

HAYES

DAMN.

The only time my dick had been harder than this moment was after an unexpected firefight with insurgents back in my SEAL days. Post-battle erections were the norm. The need to fuck intense, not that we ever had the opportunity deployed.

But even that time was nothing like this. Holy shit, not even close. Who knew small-town Montana had the hottest women on the planet? *Woman.* One of my hands cupped a perfect tit, fingers tweaking the taut nipple, the other working the sweetest, most drenched pussy. Finger fucking her was an easy go. She was as into this as I was.

Maybe more because when she breathed in my ear, "That all you got?" followed by a moan as I rubbed over her G-spot, I knew I'd met my match.

Deputy Megan Hager was fucking perfect. Gorgeous. Carried a gun. Didn't take any shit, but the way she was rolling her hips, I was sure she was going to take my dick just fine.

"I've got everything you need, doll baby."

"Don't call me that," she snapped then leaned in and bit my pec through my t-shirt.

Cum spurted into my boxers. The bite of pain mixed with the hot, tight feel of her around my fingers was my undoing. And I hadn't even fucked her yet. "I'm the one who's going to make you come in the next ten seconds. I can call you anything I want."

Her fingers gripped my biceps as I slid my thumb over her clit. She wasn't wearing her deputy uniform today, but a tank top and short skirt with easy access. I couldn't see my fingers working up into her tight, dripping heat, but I could watch her beautiful face.

Her head tipped back and thumped against the back side of the barn. It was as far as we'd made it from the barbeque at the Alpha Mountain Security compound before we got our hands on each other. It wasn't dark yet, and I could see her whiskey eyes flare then fall closed. Her lips parted. Her pussy clenched then milked my fingers. Her body tensed, and I set my hand over her mouth to stifle her moan as she came.

Yeah, she came. And came some more. Dripping her sticky honey all over my hand. When I only felt ripples around my fingers, I slipped them free, grabbed a condom from my wallet then opened my jeans.

I was getting inside of her before she was done coming. Her lids fluttered open, and her gaze dropped to the action of me rolling the latex down my length.

A bird chirped in the background. A slight breeze moved across us, but it did nothing to cool my need for Megan.

"I'm big. I got you all wet and soft. Think you can take a dick like mine?"

She licked her lips, and sweat broke out on my brow.

"Cocky much?" she countered.

"You're about to find out."

I also wanted her consent. Heavy petting was one thing. Outdoor sex, where there was a chance we might be found, was another. I'd take her back to my bed, but I lived in the bunkhouse. We had our own rooms—me, Kennedy, Taft, and now Quincy—but I had a feeling Megan didn't want anyone knowing about this. Or had any intention of staying over. Hell, it was four in the afternoon. It wasn't like I'd be making her breakfast anytime soon.

Except after wringing one orgasm from her, I knew it wasn't going to be enough. It'd been three weeks since I saw her for the first time bringing coffee with Ford's woman, Indigo. I'd been on a ladder adding security to Indi's house, and shit if I hadn't almost fallen off.

Three weeks spent circling each other. After the incident up in the mountains with the bastard who'd been involved in our SEAL teammate's murder and framing, I'd seen a shit ton of Megan. Yet this was the first time I'd gotten my hands on her. From that very first greeting, I'd known she'd wanted me just as much as I wanted her. And she sure as shit was the kind of woman who got whatever–or rather, whomever–she wanted. She was beauty-queen beautiful and full of sass. I'd been in love since the moment I'd met her. Love at first sight on my part. Lust at first sight on hers.

"Hurry," she murmured then turned away from me and set her hands on the painted wood. With her skirt still up about her waist and her hot pink panties around her ankles...

I was going to last as long as a teenager with his first glimpses of porn.

Gripping the base of my dick, I gave it a hard squeeze. When she cantered her hips back and I got my first look at her glistening and swollen pussy–and winking, snug asshole–there was no more waiting. A little foreplay was one thing, but it'd been three weeks.

Setting my hand beside hers on the freshly painted wood, I angled my body so my front was to her back, my mouth at her neck. Lining up at her entrance, I thrust deep.

She moaned and clenched around me.

"Fuck," I snarled. She was even better than I imagined. Tight. Hot. Her little ass writhed against my hips.

"Hayes," she whimpered, wiggling some more.

I pulled back, drove deep again.

"Yes," she hissed.

With my free hand, I tangled my fingers in her hair and gently tugged.

"I thought of you like this. Getting crammed full of my cock and taking it all. You were made for me, baby doll."

She was. Maybe it wasn't what I should tell a woman five seconds after I got inside her for the first time, but this was turning into an existential experience—not a quickie at a party.

I pumped in and out of her, my eyes rolling back in my head. But when it seemed like she could take everything I gave and more, I wanted deeper. Harder.

I pulled out, making her toss that heavy chestnut hair and glare over her shoulder.

I know, baby doll. I'm desperate, too.

I spun her around and hitched my forearm under one of her knees before pressing her back against the wall. "Gotta get in you deeper," I managed to say, my voice rough with need.

"Yeah," she panted, nodding. "Good."

"You okay with rough?" I asked, shoving into her without preamble. I growled at the feel. The way she could handle me.

"You know I am," she snapped like she was irritated that I wasn't giving it to her hard enough yet.

"Good." I slammed in with a snap of my hips, my body trapping hers against the wall with more force than I'd use with most women.

She wasn't most women. She was Megan. No doubt the one for me.

"Oh," she gasped, her mouth falling open in ecstasy, her head pressing back against the barn wall.

The Montana summer sun was on my bare ass, but I didn't give a shit. The world could catch fire around us and neither of us would know. All I could see was Megan. All I could feel was her perfect pussy. All I could breathe in was her soft scent. Hear her satisfied moans.

I shoved in and out of her, driving deeper, lifting her foot from the ground with each brutal stroke.

"Yes...Hayes," she moaned.

For some reason, I hated her using my call sign right now. I wanted to be *Rafael* with her–the guy I didn't even believe still existed within me. But I wanted that first-name intimacy. That connection. Which, if I wasn't balls deep in her, I'd have to think long and hard about because until her, it had never even entered my mind.

It made no sense because we hadn't even had a

date. This was clearly nothing more than a mutual scratching of an itch.

Or it was supposed to be. A quickie before we returned to the barbeque.

Her muscles tightened around my cock, and the sounds coming from her lips were incoherent syllables.

My pulse thrummed, and I breathed like I'd just swam two miles. "Is this what you need, baby doll? You want my cock nice and deep?"

"Yes...God, yes!" she cried out. She lifted then wrapped her other leg around my back, her internal muscles spasming around my cock.

"You coming without me, beautiful?" I growled, shifting to hook my other forearm under her ass, so I could bounce her over my cock while she finished.

"Yes. Gawd, yes. Hot Navy SEAL goodness," she babbled, her arms looped around my neck, her head thrown back.

She was gorgeous when she came. Nothing prettier I've ever seen.

When her inner walls stopped rippling around my dick, I pinned her against the wall and shoved in with deep, punctuated strokes. "I feel so objectified," I told her between the aggressive thrusts. She'd come twice, taken what she'd wanted from me. I wasn't a selfish lover. Hell, the woman always came first.

"Now you know how it feels," she retorted.

I laughed. Yeah, with a face that beautiful and the body to match, she probably spent her whole life deflecting men's ideas about her.

She bit my neck, hard, and I came, bucking into her, loving that animal aggression. The pleasure went on and on, black dots clouding my vision.

I filled the condom, but I didn't want to stop. I could go at least four more rounds with this hot, enigmatic beauty. As I'd suspected, I wasn't one and done with her. Far from it.

"Can I take you home?" I murmured against her shoulder, still arcing slowly in and out of her. I tried to calm my racing heart. To catch my breath, but I didn't want to. I wanted to stay in her. Deep. So fucking deep.

She shoved at my shoulders, asking to be released, and I immediately complied. Carefully, I set her on her feet and slipped from her.

"Nope, I drove my own car here." She pushed her skirt down, and when I stepped back to take care of the condom, worked her panties up her legs. "Thanks, though."

Why did she sound done with me? Her actions

showed that it was over. Seriously? Now that she got what she needed, she was already moving on? A quick fuck and then—

Yeah, I knew that was pretty much how every interaction with a sailor in port went, and I'd been okay with that. Until now. For some reason, I didn't like it with the roles reversed because I wasn't done with her. Far from it.

"I could follow." I flashed her my most charming grin. I may not have had dimples like Kennedy, but I could be damn appealing to women, too. She had wanted to fuck, after all.

Except she wasn't falling for it. For *more*.

"Nah, I'm good." She smoothed her hair then glanced up at me through her dark lashes. The scent of sex swirled around us. "I'm a big girl. I don't need to be tucked in."

"Can I take you out sometime this week?" I tried again.

Fuck if I planned on letting her walk away without making further plans.

She gave a low, sultry laugh and dropped a hand on my shoulder like we were buddies, not lovers. "Hayes, let it go. I'm not looking for romance. Only what we just did. Hot sex. You're off the hook."

She tilted her face up and went for a kiss...on my damn cheek! Seriously. My cheek.

I was kicking myself for not taking more time with her. Had I even kissed that sexy mouth yet?

Dammit! I hadn't. Her hands had been on me, sliding inside my t-shirt, unbuttoning my jeans. She'd bit my earlobe. What man could resist that?

I'd dragged my open mouth along her neck down to her shoulder, I'd sucked her pert nipple, but I'd rushed to get up that skirt and totally skipped the most intimate part.

She walked away, that ass sashaying back and forth with more swagger than a runway model.

"Can I have your number?" I called as she retreated toward her car which was parked in a field with all the others who'd come from town.

"Let it go, Hayes," she repeated in a sing-song voice like it was going to become a refrain I'd have to get used to. Like this was something she did with all the guys.

Fuck.

That.

I wasn't *all the guys*.

"Tell me this, baby doll."

Yeah, that had her turning to face me. She seemed to hate that nickname, and the way she glared had a grin spread across my face. "You liked those orgasms I just gave you? That pussy all sore and achy?"

Heat replaced frustration in her gaze, but she remained silent. She might be telling me we were one and done, but her body craved more.

"Yeah, I thought so."

She huffed then returned to her task of leaving me behind. I'd let her go.

For now.

Because it hadn't just been hot sex. It had been off the charts. Scorching.

A Navy SEAL didn't back down. If there was one thing that made an alpha male more determined to win, it was a little female rejection. Megan wanted me to chase?

Yeah, I'd chase that woman to the ends of the Earth then give her all the orgasms she could handle. Except we were both settled here in Sparks, and that made finding this woman a whole hell of a lot easier.

CHAPTER
TWO

MEGAN

"PAPERWORK WOULDN'T TAKE AS LONG if you knew how to do more than hunt and peck."

I tilted my head to glance around the computer monitor. Dan's familiar face had a wide grin.

I narrowed my eyes. "They didn't have a typing class at the academy."

He wiggled his fingers in the air as if he were a magician ready to pull a rabbit from a hat. "A semester in high school was all I needed to become a pro."

I thought of the GED I received in juvie, where

learning how to type definitely hadn't been part of the curriculum. Not that he knew anything about that. No one did since my record as a minor had been sealed.

"Everyone's got their skills," I countered. "No matter how hard I try, I'll never be as good a typist as you. I mean, you'll never be as talented a shooter as I am, so I'd say we balance each other out."

He humphed and crossed his arms over his uniform. Mary, the station manager, laughed from her desk at our banter. The phone rang, and she answered it.

"I'm a good shot," Dan muttered, dropping into his desk chair. He wasn't a huge man, but the thing squeaked with the strain. He had a few years on me, a wife, and two kids. High school sweethearts. He had everything I was never going to have, including a receding hairline. He wasn't a bad shot at all, but I did suck at typing, so I had to pick at him about something. "I finished the report for the hit and run at the quickie mart."

The place was out by the highway, and someone had clipped another car at the gas pumps while the owner was in the bathroom. There was video footage, and I had no doubt the guy from Nebraska would be getting a call from an insurance company for damages. Fortunately, we didn't have too many bad calls in Sparks, which was one of the reasons I'd returned here. A quiet, simple life. My father had left once with me in tow, and I figured he wouldn't be returning. Ever. Which was perfect for me.

I was alone here with my secrets, with my fucked up past. The older folks in town remembered when my mom left, then me and my dad, but that was it. Even Dan had been a kid when we'd left. Everyone in Sparks had been thrilled when *one of their own* returned to take the deputy job instead of some city slicker, but noone had prodded for too much more. Montanans were friendly but respected boundaries.

"Then you've got time to get me some coffee," I replied, turning back to my report on the screen. "From the Seed 'n Feed," I added. He knew the stuff that was brewed here in the break room was bad and only ingested in dire emergencies... which meant never.

I shifted in my chair. My body was sore in the best possible way, and those orgasms I received yesterday up against the side of a barn? *So good.* I was more relaxed than I'd been in a long time.

Last month, my friend Indi told me about Ford Ledger returning and setting up a security company on his family's property. Like me, he'd left town, but unlike me, he'd left to help others. In the Navy. As a SEAL.

The fact that he recruited fellow ex-SEALs to work for him had piqued my interest, along with every other single woman in town. They were all amazingly gorgeous, like right out of a Hollywood movie, but there had been something about Hayes specifically that did it for me. The chemistry between us was crazy. Better than I'd fantasized.

We'd first met when he and the others were adding a security system to Indi's house. Then we'd worked together when she'd been kidnapped on a guide trip. Hayes had worked closely with me and other law enforcement to get the family on the trip to safety then to ultimately retrieve the body of the kidnapper.

In all those times together, we hadn't even kissed. Or been in a bed.

No, he'd fucked me up against the side of a barn. Wasn't that the hottest thing ever?

My lower back was tender from where he'd pressed me against the building, and I still remember the stretch of him between my legs. God, he was big. My pussy clenched, wanting more.

He'd been everything I could ask for. Six feet of solid muscle, attentive with my body yet also rough, which was exactly how I liked it. I didn't need the roses and wine crap. I had no intention of forming a lasting relationship with my hookups. Not even the sexy ex-SEAL.

Lord knew, my life was not conducive to that. *I wasn't*. No strings was easy. Fun. Of course, men didn't usually see it that way. *They* were the ones who were supposed to walk away, to forget my name after they came. They also took one look at my face– the one I got from my long-gone beauty pageant mom–and started a whole fantasy in their heads that had absolutely nothing to do with who I really was. I might have been pretty on the outside, but not even becoming a sheriff's deputy could make them understand there was nothing soft and feminine about me, other than my pillowy lips and big baby blues.

I didn't trust men. Not for more than the few minutes it took for them to get me off. They were good for something. Sex. Not relationships and definitely not love. Because a husband was supposed to stick. Like Dan. A father was supposed to... do fatherly things, but mine sure as hell hadn't.

I wasn't falling for any man, no matter how talented his dick was.

Dan waved his finger in a little salute, which had me returning to my report and off my stupid thoughts. He asked Mary what she wanted on his way. The Seed 'n Feed had been just that, the usual farmer supply store, until Holly Martin had added on a coffee shop. Locals stopped in to buy the ranch supplies they needed and now had a place to visit.

That reminded me of my call this morning, the report I was working on now.

It'd been a welfare check at a ranch south of town. The man who ran the place was in his eighties and lived alone. He hadn't stopped by the Seed 'n Feed like he usually did every morning, and his friends had been worried. I'd gone to see if he was okay, but it turned out, he got a flat tire on the way. I turned into an auto mechanic and put on his spare. I knew how to change a tire on my own, but Mr. Dozer ensured I followed his every direction. Fortunately, the report on a welfare check that became a civilian assist wasn't all that complicated.

Neither was typing, but I wasn't going to win any awards. I had to guess Dan had a few on a shelf somewhere he polished weekly.

I was about to hit submit on the report when my computer chimed, indicating my news feed had found a match. I hit the button, not wanting to lose what I'd worked so hard to type out then switched screens to my search results. I'd set up a feed to search for references to my name, Colin Hager, Rebecca Hager, Rexford Juvenile Detention Center, and Empress Sapphire so if an Internet article or even an online magazine included those terms, I'd know.

My hand shook as if I'd had a triple espresso from the Seed 'n Feed as I clicked on the single result. It was for my dad. Dreading what I'd read, but content knowing Dan was occupied and I could skim it undisturbed, I opened it.

COLIN HAGER WAS INJURED *in a car accident on the interstate near Jefferson City, Washington. Hager, fifty-five, received minor injuries when a semi changed lanes and struck his vehicle. Per the truck driver, who was not injured, the late model sedan was in his blind spot. The truck driver was issued a citation and released at the scene.*

THE DATE of the article was three days ago.

"Great," I muttered, saving the article to a folder on an external thumb drive with everything else that came up. Not much appeared about me personally, and I hadn't seen anything about my mom in fifteen years. I figured she was still alive–otherwise, I was sure to have read an obituary–but I had no idea where she'd gone since that day she walked out on us with another man.

My dad, though, popped up on occasion. Not just on the internet searches but in my life, usually a few years in-between visits. Based on the article, he had been in eastern Washington state three days ago, which wasn't good. He was nearby, and the only reason he'd ever return to Montana and especially to Sparks was me.

CHAPTER
THREE

HAYES

"THREE MINUTES, FORTY-TWO SECONDS," Ford announced as I streaked under the last trip wire in the obstacle course. "That's your best yet."

The course had been set up so it cut through the mountain and made for a really fucking hard work-out. It was a rugged path that went up steep inclines then back down them. There were fallen logs to jump, even crossing a damned stream and all kinds of other natural obstacles. The only thing it didn't have was an ocean swim. It wasn't fun, but I was a SEAL, and if it was fun, it'd be boring.

I accepted Kennedy's high-five as I walked off the exertion, setting my hands on my hips. They'd already had their turns and were clocking us.

Taft, our youngest team member, came in behind me, his injured knee not slowing his time because he was too fucking fast, but he'd slid down the steep section and veered off course. On his ass. After a knee injury had ended his military career, he was getting stronger by the day and already lapped us all, the fucker. "Four twenty-four."

Ford tossed him his water bottle.

My new time had everything to do with the set of blue balls I'd had since hooking up with Megan three days ago. I'd never been so frustrated after being so thoroughly satisfied in my life. One taste of her, and I wasn't the same. Rubbing one out in the shower, several times a day, wasn't cutting it.

Being away the past two days on a job for Alpha Mountain had been a good distraction, but it'd also kept me away from her. Kennedy and I went to New York to pick up a VIP and play bodyguards. The diplomats had wanted extra security for a bachelor party in Vegas, so we'd spent two days babysitting. Following them around as they partied at the pool and in the high stakes section of the casino had been an easy job without any firefights, explosions or helicopter extractions.

No Megan either.

I paced and eventually caught my breath, wiping my sweaty brow with the hem of my t-shirt. "We need another barbeque. Tonight."

Kennedy rolled his eyes at my unsubtle attempt to get in front of my elusive hook-up. Elusive because she hadn't gotten back to me. Checked in with Indi about me. Nothing.

"Jesus, did you grow a vagina?" he asked.

I glared at him but knew he was right in questioning. I wasn't one to pine.

"Yeah, that must've been some pussy." Taft tilted his head back to squirt water over his face. He was sweaty and dirty, especially his back half after taking a slide down the side of the mountain.

I growled, not liking how he considered Megan to be *just* pussy.

"You asked Indi for her number. She give it to you?" Kennedy asked.

"Yeah."

"Did you call the girl? Tell her to meet you beneath the bleachers after gym class?"

Kennedy liked to push, but he was the biggest

flirt of all of us. Liked *all* the ladies. I doubted he'd know the perfect pussy if it sat on his face.

"I texted," I admitted to them. "Haven't heard back."

She worked at the sheriff's office, and I could stop in now that I was back, but even me—and my new vagina—knew that was a little extreme no matter how I felt. Showing up at a woman's work was definitely more stalker than past lover.

"Maybe she's not interested in more." Ford offered me a slow head shake of what I assumed was a mixture of disappointment and amusement at my predicament. "Women are allowed to have one-night stands."

"It wasn't one night," I snapped, wishing I'd had a whole night with her instead of a quickie that took all of fifteen minutes.

"Fine, a quick fuck. Whatever. Not all women have sensitive emotions like you do. That's all I'm saying," Ford added as if that clarified anything.

"Yeah, pathetic isn't a good look for you, bro." Kennedy flicked the front of my cap, making it fly off into the dirt.

I snapped the hat up, ran a hand over my sweaty head, then put it back in place. "Oh yeah? What would you do in my shoes, oh, Master of Women? When you make a real connection with one but she bails?"

Taft snorted. "I'm not sure I'd consider a quickie down at the barn a *real connection*, Romeo."

No one at the barbeque had missed the way we'd snuck off or how I'd been into her since the day at Indi's house when we'd first met.

I expected another jab from Kennedy, our resident man-whore, but for some reason, he slid a glance at Quincy, who seemed to be extremely interested in the hem of her jogging shorts.

She'd done the course with Kennedy and Ford earlier and had a towel slung over her shoulders, clearly not wanting to get involved in my problems.

She was the newest member of Alpha Mountain Security. She and her helicopter. While not a SEAL, she'd been in the Navy herself, hauled our asses out of sticky spots more times than I could remember. She was used to our stupid conversations. I didn't know a better pilot—man or woman—and that was why she was here. Only the best for Alpha Mountain. *Hooyah.*

The way they were acting, I had to wonder if Kennedy and Quincy had hooked up at some point.

Not in the week she'd been here but before that. While we'd been in service. Quincy was smart, and I figured she'd know better than getting mixed up with him. Kennedy was a player with a capital P, but then again, I was pining for a woman who'd fucked and fled. I wasn't one to judge, that was for sure.

"How do you know what happened at the barn?" I asked Taft. "I could've been reciting Pablo Neruda to her while she lounged on a picnic blanket near the stream."

Taft angled his head and gave me a look that screamed *get real*. "Uh-huh. So you didn't give her that SEAL ride she was looking for?"

My nostrils flared, and my brows slammed down. For some reason, that irritated the fuck out of me. Of course, I'd been as eager to give her that ride as she'd been to get it, but I hated the idea of Megan thinking of it—of me—as just a SEAL ride.

Indi strolled up, her usual hiking boots on her feet. She'd recently quit her job at the outdoor adventure company since the owner was the fucking asshole who'd told the kidnapper where she'd be in the mountains. Not on purpose but because he'd been duped. Still, no man should tell a stranger a woman's whereabouts, no matter what line he was fed.

Ford had threatened his life, and he'd bailed Sparks and most likely Montana.

Because of what had gone down, she had the motivation and support to start her own company. One whose first client was Alpha Mountain Security. Ford wanted her to help us with our wilderness skills. Not that the crew already here hadn't learned how to survive in the wild for weeks, but not everyone Ford would hire would be former SEALs. Like Quincy, to start. She was from somewhere in the south where there were no mountains. Not even winter.

"Help me out, Indi," Taft said, giving her his signature smile. "Put Hayes here out of his misery and tell him Megan's been writing her new married name—Megan Reyes—in little hearts on her notebook."

Indi's eyes sparkled as she replied, "Definitely. She told me all about it after our pillow fight."

I glared. She had mercy on me and gave me a shoulder bump. "I'm just playing with you, Hayes. Megan hasn't said a word."

I wasn't sure if that was a good thing or a sign that she really had been one and done.

"I know she was pretty interested in meeting you guys when she heard about Alpha Mountain," she added. "When you installed the security system at my house, let's say the chemistry between you two was pretty obvious. The Sparks dating pool can get pretty shallow. Believe me, I know."

Ford cleared his throat behind her, and she turned and looped her arms around his neck, instantly turning soft. "I'm not talking about you, of course," she murmured.

"You'd better not be," he said gruffly, but his hands began to roam up and down her back like he couldn't get enough of touching her. "I might take you behind the barn and—"

She covered his mouth with her hand and grinned. I'd known Ford for almost ten years, and I was seeing a whole new side to him with Indi. A side I honestly didn't know existed. She was a good thing for him because he was still up to his eyeballs in trying to root out corruption in the military.

We'd gotten a good lead from the fucker, Tully, who'd kidnapped Indi. Her brother, Buck, had gotten caught in the middle of shady US soldiers moving drugs from Afghanistan. He'd been murdered for it, to keep him quiet. Because Ford had poked around into his best friend's death, he'd been kicked out of the Navy on a bogus charge.

He was getting on with his life, building a solid

company that did similar jobs as the SEALs without the red tape, but his name hadn't been cleared yet, and whoever was in charge of the drug ring was still at large. While all of us were doing jobs for Alpha Mountain, we were on standby to deal with whoever was fucking with Ford. Kennedy's computer digging had yet to reap any results. We wouldn't stop, though, until the assholes were six feet under and Ford's honor returned.

But the silver lining of all of this was that Ford had returned to Sparks and had his second chance with Indi. Now nothing could bring him down. I guessed that was what a good woman could do for a man.

And fuck if I didn't want to experience that with my own small town spitfire. The one with the long thick brown hair and sultry eyes. The one who made a boxy deputy uniform look hotter than a thin white t-shirt under a spray of water.

"While those two have another workout" — Kennedy said as Ford and Indi veered off toward the main house to get cleaned up— "I'll check the overnight data on Tully and his known associates."

Quincy offered a little wave and took off at a jog toward the bunkhouse. She was living there with us, each in our room with a private bathroom.

The three of us followed at a slower pace. "It's been a month. Anything new?" I asked Kennedy.

He shook his head. "No. It seems the assholes behind all this are just as cagey as your woman."

I punched him in the arm then shook my head. "Asshole."

CHAPTER FOUR

HAYES

I SAW the flashing lights in the distance. Sparks had mountains all around, but the open space was vast, and it was easy to see for miles. It was the same in Albuquerque where I'd grown up, but there was something more... vast... in Montana. It was easy to pick up on weather–or trouble–well in advance.

I pulled my truck off the road a short way behind the sheriff's patrol car. The sun was high and bright, yet even so, it wasn't crazy hot this time of year like it would be in New Mexico. Not a cloud in the sky. Megan, along with her partner, were questioning a man standing by the hood of his older sedan.

Mrs. L, Ford's grandmother who lived with us on the Ledger property, asked me to pick up a dozen eggs for her, so she could make a birthday cake. She was always making baked goods for everyone in town, and I was happy to volunteer to collect them, but now she'd have to wait. No way was I leaving my woman while she handled a traffic stop. I'd let her do her thing, but I pulled my gun from the console just in case.

The guy wasn't wearing an IED strapped to his chest, but still. I protected what was mine.

Megan being a law enforcement officer made my dick hard. Yeah, everything about her did that, but the idea that she believed in justice and wanted to enforce it was plain hot. It didn't hurt that I knew what those curves felt like, the ones not well hidden beneath her brown uniform.

Her hair was pulled back into a severe bun low on her neck, but she still looked fucking amazing. After being in New York and Vegas for the body-guard/babysitting job, laying eyes on her again only made me want her even more. I knew what her body felt like, what she sounded like when she came.

I pushed that aside though because her job involved bad shit. I'd only dealt with military-grade bad stuff, but growing up on the rough city streets, I knew what went down. I wasn't stupid enough to think that Sparks was immune to wife beaters or drug problems, but that didn't mean I wanted my woman handling them.

Yeah, I had a problem. I loved that she was a ball buster with a pistol on her hip. But I also wanted to climb out of my truck, get between her and the perp they were chatting up and keep her safe. I was the SEAL. The one trained to deal with all kinds of danger. I volunteered for the Navy knowing full well my life would be at risk. Becoming a SEAL had upped the chances of my early death. I'd taken on that risk and come out alive, unlike Indi's brother, Buck.

I tensed as I heard the perp's voice raise through my open window. He was getting belligerent with Megan and her partner. It took everything in me not to draw my weapon and step forward. They had to follow procedure, but I sure as hell didn't.

Megan kept her tone even–I couldn't hear what she said, but I was sure she was laying down the law. Literally.

The perp took a wild swing at her. I reached for the door handle but stopped, transfixed by Megan's quick response. She smoothly ducked beneath the haymaker, then grabbed the guy's arm, pressing it into his torso before rolling his wrist into a lock and circling it behind his back. She lifted high, pushing his shoulder almost out of joint before he went along with her efforts and spun around, his face slamming into the hood of the car.

Fuck me, that was impressive. And it pissed me off. My protective instincts roared to life, and I had my fingers around the door handle to go take care of the fucker myself for attacking my woman, but her partner stepped in.

He was a burly guy in his thirties named Dan who was married and had kids, per Ford's grandma. He pulled his cuffs off his utility belt and slapped them on the fucker. Once secured, Megan stepped away and spoke into her walkie-talkie clipped to her shoulder, I assumed requesting backup.

I watched her chest rise and fall. From a distance, I could tell her adrenaline was pumping, but she was in control. Her gaze scanned her surroundings, and I knew the second she saw me in the distance. Her body stiffened–as if going on high alert–before her shoulders dropped. I didn't get so much as a chin tilt before she turned her back on me. Dan kicked the man's feet wide, and he frisked the guy, keeping one hand on the back of his head.

Five minutes later, a second patrol car–backup–

arrived with lights and siren. The guy was loaded into the back and driven off just as a tow truck pulled over. I recognized the name on the side– Lander's Auto Shop–from the place in town. Ford knew the guy. Hell, he knew everyone in town since he'd been raised here.

As Lee Landers and Dan worked on getting the car hooked up, Megan strode my way. Her stride was long, and her gaze focused on me. My dick hardened at the way she stared at me. Pissed and intent. I had to shift in my seat to get comfortable because I was having visions of her telling me I'd been bad and needed to be frisked, cuffed, and thoroughly inter-rogated.

I set my forearm on the open window as she stepped close and leaned down.

"What are you doing here?" she asked.

I liked a woman to be excited to see me, not pissed off, but with Megan, I had to take what I could get.

"Driving into town."

"Most people don't stop and watch the show."

"Impressive show," I replied, my gaze roving from her eyes to her lips then back.

She glanced toward the car that was being pulled onto the flatbed then back at me.

"Not everyone is cooperative."

"Good thing I was here. Just in case."

Her eyes narrowed, and a lesser man would feel his balls shrivel. Her gaze snagged on my gun. "I don't need your protection."

Arguing wouldn't get in her bed, so I said, "You think I'm going to come upon you with a perp and just drive on by?"

I didn't know what kind of men she dealt with, but a real man would make sure a woman was safe. Even if she had a trained partner. And a gun. And cuffs. And years of experience.

Since she was *my* woman, it was best she learned now I was a protective mofo. Because she *was* my woman. She just didn't know it yet.

"What time is your shift over?" I changed the topic.

Her dark brow quirked. "A half an hour ago. Why?"

I gave a negligent shrug as I shifted my left hand to the steering wheel. "Just wondering what time to be at your house."

She studied me then sighed. "Look, Hayes. We had fun."

"That adrenaline pumping through your blood right now? I bet it's made your nipples hard. A rough fuck is a great way to bleed all that energy off."

Her lips twitched as she cocked her head. I knew what that cinnamon-colored hair looked like long and wild, and it only made her buttoned-down deputy look even sexier. "Your dick volunteering?"

A grin slowly spread across my face. "I'm volunteering more than my dick. I'm good with my hands... and mouth, too."

Heat flared in her eyes, even briefly.

"Just sex?" she asked after a long pause. Her question made it clear that she had zero interest in any kind of relationship. That me getting in her bed meant I was getting right back out when I was done satisfying her with my volunteer dick.

"I don't plan to rearrange your closets," I countered. This wasn't just sex, but I wasn't going to tell her that now. She was agreeing, and she'd be more pliant beneath me. A few orgasms had women changing their minds about anything. Hell, if she got those full lips wrapped around my dick, I'd give her the world.

She huffed, and a smile turned up the corner of those perfect lips. "Fine. My address is–"

"I know where you live." Kennedy wasn't the only one with mad computer skills. And Sparks wasn't a big town. I could have gone door to door and found her if I had to. Or asked Mrs. L.

"We'll follow the tow into town, check in with the deputies who took the guy to be processed, then clock out."

"My dick and I will be waiting." I reached down and shifted my junk. Her dark eyes followed the action, and she licked her lips. *Fuck. This woman.*

CHAPTER
FIVE

MEGAN

MY DICK *and I will be waiting.* That was all I could think about as I drove home from the station. I was... irked by Hayes because he was too good-looking for my own good. When I'd caught a glimpse of him in his truck parked behind the scene, just watching, my heart leaped into my throat.

Which pissed me off. More than the drunk taking a pop swing at me had. I didn't want to be excited to see Hayes. I didn't want to *want* him again.

But I did. Even after three days. And he knew it.

I didn't even like him having that bit of control over me. Pressing me into a barn and fucking me hard was one kind of control. Telling me my nipples were hard and I needed some D to take the edge off was another.

As I pressed the button to shut my garage door behind me–with more effort than necessary–I gave myself a little pep talk. "He has a big dick. You like a big dick. They're useful, which means he's useful. You don't have to keep him, Megan. Use him and lose him."

I pushed open the door to the kitchen and instinctively reached for my weapon even though I knew it was Hayes. I'd seen his truck parked out front and noted my security system was offline.

He took up too much of the small room with his big SEAL size and just the sight of him made my ovaries perk up.

"Use him and lose him, baby doll?"

"Jesus. Don't you know not to break into a law enforcement officer's house? How'd you get past my security system anyway?" I shook my head as I went to the kitchen cabinet beside the sink and pulled down my small gun safe. Setting it on the counter, I punched in the code. I only gave him a cursory glance because any more and I'd climb him like a tree. He'd been right, dammit. The adrenaline from the call had me wanting him.

Or maybe it was his clean scent. Or his bulging muscles. Dark brown hair. Strong jaw. Big dick I knew he was packing. The dick. Focus on the dick!

"Don't insult a SEAL. Your alarm is good, but I'm better."

I looked his way and rolled my eyes.

"Don't see many family pictures on the fridge or mantel," he commented.

"It's just me," I replied. Wasn't he here for sex, not personal questions?

"Sorry to hear your parents are dead," he said.

The softness of his voice had my gaze lifting to meet his. "They're not dead."

He blinked and opened his mouth, probably to ask the one thing I would never get into with him. The topic I didn't discuss with anyone. I remembered the article I'd read about my dad and how he was probably headed this way. I frowned.

"You're here for sex, right?" I pulled my gun from my holster and tucked it into the safe–along with any thoughts about my father–then shut it and put it away in the cabinet. I'd learned how to keep my emotions in check when I was seventeen. It was safer that way with everyone, but I had a feeling if Hayes started poking around, he'd find what he was looking for. Better to play indifferent than anything else. Forgettable.

It was easier to keep him away than to let him in and have him walk away. Because he would once he learned the truth.

Everyone walked away from me. It was better that I did it first.

"You're in a foul mood," he pointed out. "I know what can fix that."

"I know. A few orgasms." I tugged the bottom of my uniform shirt from the pants. I wasn't as into fashion as my mom had been, but even I knew brown was not a good color on any woman. Especially in polyester.

"Those, definitely. I was talking about something else."

I arched a brow as I worked the buttons open. Hayes' eyes followed my action very closely. My bulletproof vest and undershirt appeared and were far from sexy.

"Control, baby doll. Hand it over."

I shrugged off the shirt and tossed it on the kitchen table. Next, I worked the velcro straps on my vest then added it to the pile. A sigh escaped with the heft of it gone.

"What are you talking about?"

"How many calls did you go on today?"

I shrugged then stared at the ceiling to think. "A domestic, served papers, an auto assist and one arrest."

"Besides the slugger from earlier?"

"No. He's the arrest for the day."

"You must be tired. Your *brain* must be tired."

Turning to the fridge, I opened the door and snagged a beer. Holding it up, I asked without words if he wanted one. He shook his head.

I shut the door, popped the top, and took a healthy swig.

"My brain's fine."

His brown-eyed gaze circled my face again. "Sure is. If I told you to go take a shower, what would happen?"

"I'd tell you I was going to do that anyway."

He pushed off the counter where he'd been leaning and closed the space between us. To keep meeting his gaze, I had to tip my head back. He took the beer from my fingers. "Go shower like a good girl, and I'll give you a reward."

If he didn't look so damn sexy with his lips quirked and his piercing gaze, I might have punched him in the jaw for the *good girl* comment alone, much less for ordering me about.

It seemed Hayes had a bit of a kink. He wanted to call me *baby doll* and *good girl*. Ha. I was so far from being his good girl, it was laughable.

That didn't dampen my interest in him, though. Oddly, it heightened it. I might not be the girl he thought I was, but that wasn't going to stop me from enjoying the ride.

Literally.

Full of snark, I replied, "A reward? Like candy? Something to suck on and lick, maybe?"

He took me by the shoulders, spun me to face the living room, and gave my ass a little swat. "Like me joining you in the shower to suck on and lick your pussy."

Oh. I stumbled envisioning him on his knees and doing just that. My panties dampened.

"I'm going," I said. "Not because you told me to but because I do want that reward."

I heard his laugh and footsteps follow as I entered my bathroom. "I thought you might. If someone needs to have her pussy licked, it's you, Megan Hager."

I flipped on the spray, set the temperature, then turned to face him. He was in the open doorway, his head almost reaching the top of the frame. Hot. This guy was definitely the hottest I'd had. Everything about him was hot–even the bossy, over-protective alpha male bit. Maybe especially that part.

"What are you insinuating? That I'm wound up? That I'm uptight? I'll have you know Dan's wife isn't calling him any of those things after a long shift."

His only response was him scratching his cheek with a finger. Why didn't he get riled and angry? "I'm sure Dan's wife's got her lips wrapped around his dick right now, clearing his mind of everything but nutting in her mouth."

I winced, not wanting to think of my partner in that way. "Nice."

"I've been away for work. Two days playing body-guard in Vegas. In that time, I wondered how sweet you'd be. Do you want me to eat your pussy because I sure as hell want to find out."

Of course, I wanted my pussy licked. And eaten. He knew it. He knew I knew. Saying no only made me look stupid and unsatisfied. Mulishly, I answered. "Yes."

He laughed, his head tipped back which only made me want to throat punch him.

"That was hard for you, wasn't it? Giving up even that little bit of control."

I frowned. I'd never really thought about it before, but yeah. I didn't like being told what to do.

Going along blindly only got me a year in juvie. I'd learned the hard way once, I wasn't falling for it a second time.

"I don't know you," I replied. "And I don't trust you."

"Reasonable," he countered, being... reasonable. "Cautious is smart. But know this. I wouldn't do anything to hurt you or shame you when we're together. Know that I'll be watching out for you the whole time. That you're safe with me."

Wow. It sounded good, but I wasn't lying when I said I didn't trust easily.

"Okay. How about baby steps?" He came into the room and reached for my undershirt. I let him–*let him*–lift it over my head and drop it on the floor. "Shower. If you can obey me in that, I'll join you and get my face between those creamy thighs."

I stripped off the rest of my clothes and did as he wanted without saying anything else. He remained where he was and watched. And I watched his gaze go from attentive to heated as I stood before him bare then turned and stepped in. He could see me through the glass door as I soaped up, then washed my hair.

"I thought you were coming in," I called.

"Enjoying the view, baby doll. Enjoying the

view." His hand went to the front of his jeans, and in that moment, I felt powerful. This big—no, huge—guy wanted me. His dick was hard for me. He'd had a lot of women, I was sure.

Which I appreciated. I sure as hell didn't like to train a man.

My hands stilled in my hair and realized this must've been what my mother felt like. Using her beauty to snag a man.

The door slid open and in stepped Hayes. Naked. I must've been distracted by my deadbeat mother longer than I thought if I missed him undressing. God, he was gorgeous. Sculpted. Fit in a way I'd never seen before. His skin was tan and sprinkled with dark hair. A thatch of it was on his chest, between dark, flat nipples that tapered to his navel then into a thin line down to his dick.

It was erect and curved upward, bobbing against his belly. It was a darker color than the rest of him, his balls large and pendulous. A guy's dick wasn't usually all that attractive, but Hayes was big everywhere. No wonder I'd been sore for a few days.

He gripped the base and gave himself an easy pump without a hint of modesty.

"This is just sex, Hayes," I reminded him. "And

it's going to be pretty hard to have it in my small shower. You're too big."

"I fit in you perfectly, and you know it."

"I'm not talking about my pussy," I countered.

"I am." He pointed to the back wall, and I shifted in that direction. He settled beneath the spray, then dropped to his knees. Taking my ankle, he lifted it up and over his back, so my thigh rested on his shoulder.

He grunted in clear satisfaction as his gaze centered on my pussy. I shaved and tended to the area, but I didn't go bare. I'd tried waxing once and hated it. I wasn't a masochist. If Hayes was hoping for a Brazilian he'd be–

"Prettiest pussy ever."

Huh.

His dark eyes flicked up my body. Held mine. "Time for a taste. I bet you're as sweet as I've been imagining."

I frowned even as my pussy clenched with anticipation. "I'm not sure what about me gave you that idea."

His palms slid up my inner thighs, and his thumbs parted me. Then he licked.

"Oh fuck," I called into the steamy air because he hadn't given me a sexy little swipe. No. He'd used his shoulder to push my thigh higher, and that had him able to lick me from asshole to clit. I'd never had anyone put their tongue there before—my back entrance, not my clit—and holy shit, it had been electrifying. When he slipped a finger into me and sucked on my clit, I was a goner. Close to coming in seconds.

When my foot was slipping on the tub, he lifted the other leg over his shoulder too, and I was caught. Pinned between Hayes' large body, his mouth and the tile.

My fingers tangled in his wet hair as I writhed on him then clenched as I came because he'd not only fucked a finger into my pussy, but carefully slid one into my ass, at least partway. That bold action, where it had been unexpected and without any gentle finesse, had pushed me over the edge. I cried out his name as I came and came. He didn't let up, tugging on my clit and curling a thick finger over a magical spot inside me until I was wrung out, thankful he was holding me up.

"Just sex, Hayes," I murmured, realizing I was in big trouble here. A thirty-second orgasm and a finger in the ass. I could get used to it.

His fingers stilled then slipped from me. The next thing I knew, the shower was off, I was over his shoulder and tossed onto my bed. Dripping wet.

I was in a far from seductive pose, legs spread, but awkwardly, and I pushed up on an elbow.

"Just sex? This is how I do *just sex*. Rough. Wild. No holding back. Think you can handle that?"

I couldn't help but lick my lips and nod because all of that sounded really good. Especially coming from a guy as perfectly formed, as perfectly rugged and manly as Hayes.

"I like to be in control, baby doll." He held up his hand. "I think you like it, too. Your pussy's wet. I can see it from here. You were creaming all over my face." He brought a finger to his mouth and sucked on it. "Tastes fucking good, too."

"Hayes."

"I won't ever do something you don't want. You don't like it, you tell me. But don't lie and say you don't like me in charge when it comes to sex because I know otherwise."

I snapped my mouth closed because he was right. I'd already come. He hadn't.

"Fine."

"Fine from a woman means anything and every-thing but *fine*. Say *yes, Hayes, I want you in charge*."

I looked at the ceiling and gave a humorous

laugh. This was what I got for craving a guy like Hayes.

Of course, he wasn't doing anything wrong except coming up alongside all my insecurities and hot buttons and pushing every one. But I didn't care. Ultimately, I was still in charge. He may think he was getting a submissive baby doll, but I was getting what I needed.

"Yes, Hayes, I want you in charge," I lied.

Or maybe it wasn't a lie—at least not for these sixty seconds.

He nodded once then stalked toward me, taking a gentle hold of my ankle and pulling me close. "Now, the one thing we didn't do the other day, or earlier, is kiss. I want those lips, baby doll."

I put a hand on his chest when he crawled up over me and shook my head. "I told you, I'm not your baby doll."

His eyes crinkled. "You did, didn't you?" He slanted his mouth over mine and slid his lips ever so slowly over it. I was expecting rough. I thought he'd be quick with the tongue. But he took his time. The unexpected softness set off flutters in my belly. He continued to taste me this way, with soft exploration, even while every other part of him—particularly the part I wanted most between my legs–was hard and insistent.

I lost my breath, looping my arm behind his neck to deepen the kiss. Kisses often bored me, but there was nothing boring about Hayes or the size of him above me. I liked his focus. The intensity. The way he went slow and soft enough for me to register every tiny nuance.

"Mmm." He rubbed his lips when we broke apart. "That was even better than I imagined."

He'd imagined kissing me? For some reason, it seemed out of place with the guy who'd shoved me up against the barn wall and screwed me senseless. Out of place but not disappointing.

Still, I wasn't going to go soft and senseless on him. "You going to kiss me all night, or can I get some action around here?"

In a flash, Hayes had my wrists pinned beside my head and his knee shoving my thighs wide. I arched against him, not to fight the restraint, but to get more of my skin in contact with his.

"Come on, Hayes. Show me what you've got," I dared.

"It's Rafael."

"What?"

"My name. Call me Rafael. Or Raf for short."

Rafael. It suited him–strong and protective. "Show me, Raf." I rolled my hips up to meet his.

He lowered his head, and I rolled my eyes when it seemed like he was coming in slow for another kiss, but he bit my lower lip and pulled it between his teeth before releasing it with a pop.

I gasped, my core gushing at the mixture of pain and pleasure.

Hell, yeah. Rafael definitely knew how to give it just the way I liked it.

He paused and studied me, his dark eyes roving over my face. Then he nipped my neck and lower to flick his tongue over my nipple.

"This is just sex," I blurted. I didn't know what made me say it–the offer of his first name, maybe?-- but it was the wrong moment.

Hayes lifted his head and fixed me with a glower. "Oh, you've made that abundantly clear, baby doll." Something in the dark gleam of his eyes made me think he intended to punish me for it.

He released my wrists and pushed back, and for one infuriating moment, I thought he intended to leave me like that. But he pointed a finger at me and said, "Don't move, I'm getting a condom."

I must've been out of my mind with desire because I didn't move–not even a twitch. Obedience definitely wasn't my thing, but it seemed Hayes could call the shots when I was this far gone. And he *was* getting a condom, which meant he planned to protect us both. And get his dick inside me, which was *just sex.*

Hayes stalked to the bathroom where he'd left his clothes and opened the condom as he returned. He had it rolled on and ready by the time he'd climbed back over me.

"Good girl."

"Am I?" I wasn't fishing for approval, I was trying to figure out if he was still pissed about my *just sex* edict. I didn't know why I cared. It didn't matter if he was pissed or not—it didn't change the fact that we weren't going to start dating any time soon.

"Tell me something, deputy." Hayes still had that wicked gleam in his eye as he pinioned both my wrists in one of his hands and lined his cock up with my entrance with the other.

I licked my lips. "What's that, sailor?"

His lips twitched. He fed his length into me, inch by inch, slowing when I needed a second to get used to his size. Once he'd filled me, he eased back and gave it to me with a little thrust. "You like riding this cock?"

I hid my smile. "It's adequate."

He shoved into me harder. "Adequate, huh?"

My eyes rolled back in my head with pleasure. Okay, it was way more than adequate. It was freaking awesome. If I had to rate it on a scale from one to ten, it would be a sixteen. It obviously wasn't just his cock. It was everything about Hayes. The cocky, arrogant way he handled me and my body.

"Uhn." I threw my head back on the pillow as he plowed deep into me, the headboard smacking the wall. "More than adequate," I managed.

"So, it's just sex, but the sex is good?" He trailed his thumb down my cheek and lower where he lingered with it caged lightly around my throat. It wasn't threatening, but it was possessive, and it turned my insides to liquid fire.

"Yeah, the sex is good," I panted, rocking my hips in rhythm with his to take him even deeper.

"So we'll keep it just sex," he said, alleviating the concern I had that he was going to push for more.

"Yes, great." It was a wonder I could speak at all with how fast I was losing my mind.

"On the regular."

A chuckle rocketed from my throat right before my scream of pleasure. Hayes had found my clit with his thumb, and he rubbed it while he continued to glide in and out of me. I let out a keening cry when he didn't stop, my internal muscles clenching and squeezing around his cock.

"That's right, baby doll. Come all over my dick. I'm the guy who's going to keep you happy."

Damn the arrogant bastard if I didn't come again, even harder. Or maybe it was all one long drawn out orgasm—I didn't know. All I knew was that it wiped my mind of all thought. All pressure. All reality.

I was hurtling through outer space while Hayes pounded out his own orgasm, but he still managed to wring more ripples of release from me.

There was another kiss that started off soft and ended hard and demanding, and then Hayes pulled out and pushed off, like the sailor he was. I rolled to one side and watched as he covered me with a sheet, then got up, rid himself of the condom and dressed.

"I'll see you tomorrow night." It was a statement, not a question, and he delivered it with a wink.

I opened my mouth to protest, but he shut me up by leaning over to give me another hard kiss.

"Thanks, deputy. I needed that."

He left. Just as I'd wanted. Just sex. No snuggling. No sleeping over. My orgasm still made my body tingle. The sweat on my skin hadn't even cooled.

I waited until I heard the front door close behind him before I murmured, "Yeah, me too, sailor."

CHAPTER SIX

HAYES

"WHERE ARE MY EGGS?" Mrs. L asked when I came through the back door of the main house, built by the woman herself, along with her husband back when they were newlyweds. Lots of changes had occurred since then, like Mr. Ledger passing on, but plenty stayed the same. Like the vintage linoleum floor and appliances. There was a modern commercial kitchen in the bunkhouse that had been designed to feed many mouths at once, but Mrs. L stuck to hers. The scent of lemon and vanilla clung to the warm air.

I stopped short at the older woman's question,

then my neck heated when I remembered the sole reason I'd gone into town in the first place. Eggs for her cake. Not spectacular sex with Megan.

I glanced at the clock on the wall. Three hours had passed. Three hours and no eggs.

I let the screen door slap behind me, and I tucked my hands in my pockets. "I forgot them."

There was no other answer besides the truth although fiercely edited. I'd forgotten them because I'd been balls deep in the most stubborn, prickly, and incredible woman I ever met.

Mrs. L hmphed and grabbed a plastic dome from the counter. "I figured as much and made lemon bars instead." She set the lid on a blue base that had a plate loaded with yellow squares dusted with powdered sugar and secured it closed.

I was feeling like the biggest asshole until she looked up and gave me a smile. Then winked. "Run into a certain deputy?"

My ears went hot. "Yes, ma'am."

Mrs. L was like my nana–she saw everything. As much as my family tried to protect our matriarch from knowing a faction of her family had organized as Albuquerque's drug lords–which was the reason my parents had sent me off to the Navy the day I graduated high school—she knew. She'd always known everything.

"You're perfect for her, Hayes." Her voice was soft as the grandmotherly look.

"Perfect for who?" Kennedy asked, coming into the kitchen. He grabbed a lollipop from the jar on the counter. I seriously didn't know how he kept those teeth so healthy and gleaming white considering how much sugar he ate.

The security company's command center was still in Mrs. L's sewing room. It would be finished soon in the converted barn—the one I'd screwed Megan against—but in the meantime, Kennedy and all his equipment had taken over most of the lower floor of the house. Mrs. L embraced it along with anything else that came up.

I knew after her husband—Ford's grandfather— passed away, she'd been alone here on the property for a few years. Ford's forced departure from the Navy and return had been good for her. Having all of us here certainly kept her busy although I'd never met a woman who had her hands in more things than Mrs. L.

"Megan Hager," Mrs. L said. "They spent the afternoon together."

Kennedy's red brow arched. "That so?"

I scratched the back of my neck. I was twenty-eight years old and felt like I'd been caught sneaking in after curfew.

"You should take her to dinner," she continued. "No, bring her here for dinner. I'll make a pot roast."

My mouth watered, but I gave her a look. She knew that was my favorite meal she made. "You're playing dirty," I told her.

"Ford found his woman although those two took almost ten years to figure things out. I take you to be smarter than my grandson." Mrs. L leaned toward the window over the sink and looked out. "Don't tell him I said that."

I couldn't help but laugh. She made me miss my Nana. "No, ma'am. But you're right. I am smarter."

"Then bring her to dinner."

I shook my head. "Megan wants to take things... slow." As in non-existent.

Mrs. L pursed her lips and nodded. "That makes sense."

"Sense how?"

Mrs. L was in her seventies and had lived in Sparks her entire life. Her husband had been in the military, served in Vietnam, but she'd stayed and waited for him to return. She knew everyone in town and was in every activity possible. If there was a stone that needed turning, Mrs. L would point it out and already know what lay beneath.

Going to the counter, she collected a pile of white napkins and set them on top of the cake holder. "She's... cautious."

I went to the fridge and grabbed the pitcher of tea. I poured myself a glass as I spoke, trying to keep things light. I didn't want to ask too pointed questions, but I wanted answers. Megan trusted me with her body, but if I had any chance of opening up her heart or seeing inside that head of hers, I needed a little help. "It's smart she's careful because of her job and all. She's good at it. Saw her on a traffic stop today. She's been with the department five years?"

"Oh, I'd say at least that. Closer to eight. She went to the academy in Missoula for a little while."

"College?" I asked.

"Not that I know of," she replied, which meant no.

Mrs. L looked to the back door at the sound of footsteps on the porch. Ford came in, and he took in the three of us. "We're talking about Megan Hager. She went to the police academy when she was nineteen?"

Ford looked my way. "I think she's two years younger than I am. I was already a SEAL by the time she was nineteen. She lived here all her life except for that training."

Mrs. L shook her head. "No, her father took her to Seattle for a few years. She didn't graduate from Sparks High School—I'm on the graduation committee, so I'd remember, even one about ten years ago. She came back after the academy."

Ford grabbed an apple from the bowl on the table and took a bite. "Huh, I had it wrong then."

"Her parents are here in Sparks?" I asked, even though I knew otherwise.

Mrs. L sighed. "Her mother's long gone. Left when Megan was a girl. As for her father? That man... well, no. To answer your question, no. He's not in Sparks." She fiddled with the napkins and the cake holder. "Colin Hager was a man always out for something better. He liked those... those get rich quick schemes. Maybe that's why her mother left, but what woman leaves her child? Some people I'll never understand."

From what I've heard about them, I didn't like either of her parents. But Megan had been raised by her dad. The tone of Mrs. L's voice said she wasn't wild about the man, and I trusted her judgment. The way she'd said she was alone made me assume she didn't like the guy either. Many kids hated their parents. That wasn't anything new.

A timer dinged on the stove.

"What are you cooking now?" Ford asked, patting his stomach, even though he was mostly finished with the apple.

"Nothing," she replied, turning the buzzer off. "That's my reminder I need to leave. Esther Wilson's daughter's baby shower."

"I'll help you carry everything to the car." Kennedy picked up the cake holder and held the screen door for her. She grabbed her cloth bag and keys and followed him. She glanced at me over her shoulder.

"You're not getting a lemon square, Kennedy," she called then turned to me. "You know, I can help with Megan."

Ford chuckled and studied the wood floor.

"Do I look like I need help with the ladies?" I set my hand on my chest. I didn't seem to have much trouble getting into Megan's bed, but staying there was something else. She'd given me a few minutes to recover from the mind-blowing orgasm before she kicked me out.

Mrs. L's shrewd eyes raked over me. "None of you

struggle with the ladies. I said I can help with *Megan.*
Do you want any woman, or do you want Megan?"

Wow. Okay. Consider me schooled. Her tone
made it clear there was a distinction between the
two. Sure, Megan was a woman, but Mrs. L wanted to
make sure she was *the* woman.

"I want Megan," I said. I wanted her any way I
could get her. In that bulletproof vest or bare.
Cursing my name or crying it out as she came.

Mrs. L nodded. "Good."

She followed Kennedy to her car, leaving me
with Ford.

"You better want the woman," Ford advised.
"Gram won't like her being toyed with."

I knew he was warning me of his grandmother's
potential wrath, but he was questioning my inten-
tions. And my honor.

"She's mine," I said. I'd never been more sure.
Ford nodded like he understood. There was nothing
else that could make it clearer than those two words.
I'd even use the help of a geriatric busybody to make
it happen.

CHAPTER
SEVEN

MEGAN

"I WANT to hear all about your new man." Holly waggled her eyebrows from behind the counter at the Seed 'n Feed.

I looked left and right and hoped no one I knew in town was listening in. Who was I kidding? I knew everyone in town, and they were *always* listening. Fortunately, it was quieter than her usual rush time, closer to lunch than breakfast.

A small clump of ranchers were at their usual table in the corner, but they weren't paying me any attention.

I leaned across the counter. "Hush."

She grinned and held up a can of whipped cream. "Want this on top?"

"An iced mochaccino without whipped cream? I'll check my books, but I think it's illegal."

She held the spray can against her chest. "Then spill."

I frowned. "No tip for you," I grumbled then shook my head with a laugh.

She grabbed my cup from the worn surface–it'd been the original grain counter back in the day–and angled the can over it to mound a pile of the deliciousness on top.

"How do you know anything about me and the man anyway?"

She pushed my drink toward me. "Seriously? This place has better gossip than Mrs. L."

Holly's family had owned and run the Seed 'n Feed for generations, but the coffee shop had been her brainchild.

"My love life is town gossip?" I screeched.

She shook her head, then when the bell above the door jangled, she tipped her head that way. "Got it from that one."

I looked to the door and in came Indi and Quincy, the new addition to the Alpha Mountain Security team I met at the barbeque. The one where

Hayes and I chose to have sex behind the barn instead of socializing.

"You called them to join us?"

Indi came up and gave me a quick hug. "We want facts, and the only way to do that is to catch you on your lunch break."

She knew me too well.

Quincy gave me a little wave–I didn't take her for a hugger–and added, "I'm along for the ride."

"Speaking of rides, I'm Holly, and you have the coolest ride in town."

"Quincy. And thanks. Come out, and I'll take you up sometime."

Holly's eyes lit up like it was Christmas morning, and she found her stocking full.

"Free drinks for you."

Quincy laughed as Holly grabbed the pre-made wraps from the refrigerated display case. As she did that, Indi led me and Quincy to a table in the corner. I carried my drink and took a sip.

"Don't waste any time." Holly set plates in front of us. She sat as well, facing the door in case anyone came in. "I want *all* the dirty details. The dirtier the better."

Indi's and Quincy's gazes swiveled to mine.

"It's just a fling."

Indi narrowed her eyes and held up a hand as Quincy took a bite of her turkey wrap. "Wait. You said *it's,* not *it was.* Present tense. Meaning more than the barbeque."

I look behind me then lean in. They lean in, too. "Hayes has... stopped by."

"That's..." Quincy stops to think. "Hot."

I nod.

Holly fanned her face with a hand. "She's right. That is so hot. All of them are hot, dang it. Every one of those guys is tastier than my chocolate cake. Taft's too young for me, but Kennedy?"

She made a sound like she was having a mini-orgasm just thinking about him.

I couldn't miss the way Quincy's spine stiffened, but she remained silent and took a huge bite of her sandwich.

I was pretty sure Indi noticed too but didn't say a word. She only dug into her lunch as well.

"Fine," Holly replied. "It's been five days. *Five days* of sex. With Hayes. Does he speak Spanish to you? Does his dick speak Spanish?"

I practically choked on my sandwich at her absurd question.

"I don't know if he speaks Spanish or not–"

"He does," Quincy offered.

"–because we've–"

"You've kept his mouth busy doing other things," Indi finished.

I chuckled because she was so right.

Holly cocked her head to the side. "You act like this is a bad thing. A sexy SEAL rocking my world? I wouldn't look so... grumpy." She gasped. "Don't tell me he's bad in bed, and that's why you look like you do. Please tell me that face isn't because you're orgasmless."

They all looked at me.

"No. He's good. God, really good." Was it hot in here? "He's very thorough. Totally ladies first."

Indi nodded. "Ford's like that, too. It's as if he's on a mission when we get in bed, and the end result is me fucked into unconsciousness."

"I hate you," Holly muttered, crossing her arms over her chest.

Indi gave a small smile and shrugged, completely content with being hated.

"Hayes is a great guy. What's wrong?" Quincy asked.

I barely knew her, and she knew nothing of my past.

"I'm not looking for a relationship."

"What's wrong with him stopping by every night?

Is he pushing you for more?"

I shrugged. "No, I told him outright it was just sex. He agreed."

"But?" she prodded.

"But it's hard to stick with that when he's so good."

"Good in bed or just good in general?" she asked.

"Both. Hayes is a good guy, and I don't want that."

They frown in unison. "You don't want a good guy?" Holly asked. "Color me totally confused."

"A good guy is great. I mean, who wants to be with an asshole? But he's too good. Honorable."

"That he is," Quincy explained. "No one goes into the SEALs without a core of... justice. Of a clear distinction between right and wrong. Their job is to take out the bad guys. To protect the good."

"You're a deputy," Holly pointed out. "What's the difference? You're helping people, too. Sure, you're not doing HALO jumps or blowing up buildings, but it's the same thing."

Was it? I didn't think so, and the three of them wouldn't understand. I went into law enforcement because I'd had plenty of time in juvie–alone–to realize my dad never had my back. My mother was long gone and never cared about me. The only talents I had were felonies in most states. I'd had to turn my life around and make something of myself.

Set boundaries and be on the right side of the law. To do the right thing. Because doing the wrong thing only got me abandoned.

I couldn't tell any of them that. No one here in Sparks knew my sordid secret.

"I'm not girlfriend material."

Indi frowned. "That's bullshit. You're a guy's *dream* girlfriend."

Holly nodded.

"Why? Because I've got the beauty-queen face?"

"Well, no," Indi sputtered.

"See, that's what men think. They take one look at this mug and think they know me. They make up some fantasy girl and slap my face on the top and think they've found heaven." I shook my head. "That's not me."

"I think Hayes sees the real you," Quincy said. "I mean, I don't think he was looking for the girl next door. My sense is that he likes a strong woman."

I turned my coffee cup in a circle. Quincy was right. Hayes did see the real me. Which honestly was the part that scared me the most. I'd learned to live without depending on anyone after having both parents leave me high and dry. I wasn't about to start relying on someone now.

"Maybe," I said noncommittally. "But I'm not interested in a relationship. Sex is easy. No talking–in English or Spanish–and no feelings get involved."

Quincy laughed. "Good luck with that. When those men set their sights on something they want–bad guy or hot woman–nothing's going to get in their way."

"Amen to that," Indi added.

Great. I was in really big trouble because my words and my security system weren't getting in his way.

CHAPTER
EIGHT

MEGAN

I PULLED into my garage after work. After my lunch with the girls, there had been a hit-and-run on the highway that ended with two locals in the hospital. That was the downside of law enforcement in a small town. You knew everyone, which meant every tragedy hurt. There was no separation.

Usually, after a shift like this, I wanted a cold beer, a shower, and mindless reality TV. But over the past five days–I'd definitely been keeping count–Hayes had shown up and fucked every thought from my head. I'd even let him be in control because he was able to make me forget everything and only feel.

Boy, did I feel. Hayes was a talented lover. Skilled. Inventive. Completely uninhibited and somehow picked up on every possible thing that made me hot. Dirty talk. Butt stuff. Restraints. I had no idea I had a little kink in me, but in the past five days we'd explored it all.

Not all because the man was *really* inventive. That made me eager for more.

Wasn't it also really annoying though? I'd told him just sex. No strings. He'd followed through on that, fucking me into delicious soreness and lethargy then leaving.

Yeah, he fucked and fled, just as I'd wanted.

Except he kept coming back for more.

And more. Just like I'd told the girls, nothing seemed to get him to stop.

He was as insatiable as I was. As eager. And content with nothing more than a string of simple sex.

Except it wasn't simple, and I craved more. And him. That was the problem. I liked him. His consistency. His breaking into my house, proving that nothing was going to stop him.

I closed the garage door and lifted my hand to turn the knob to my house. Then froze.

The alarm was off-line. My heart skittered, and I couldn't help but smile. He was here. Earlier than usual. Perfect... because I wanted to be bent over my kitchen counter and taken hard.

I should be pissed that he could bypass my state-of-the-art security system. I'd told him off. Once. But he'd been insulted and told me, "The day I can't breach an alarm is the day you bury me at sea."

Since then, I let it go. He wasn't here to fuck with me. No, he was here to *fuck me.*

What I found inside wasn't Hayes with a big dick and a control complex a mile wide.

No, there was a balding man sitting at my kitchen table, sipping on a beer from my fridge.

I pulled my revolver from my holster and aimed it at his head, not because he was a stranger but because I knew him all too well. "I told you not to ever come here."

My father ignored the gun and my unwelcoming words. "Hey, Meggie." He looked me up and down. "You look great."

My upper lip curled. If there was one thing I'd been told far too often in my life, it was how pretty I was. I'd heard it so much it had become an instant piss-off for me.

"You look like shit." It was true. He had one arm in a sling and cuts and bruises on his face and arms, presumably from the car accident I'd read about. Otherwise, he looked like himself although older. Smoking had made his face more lined.

He was an aging jewel thief who hadn't thought twice about letting his seventeen-year-old daughter take the fall for the job he pulled her into. It'd been about five years since I'd seen him last. Since the last time he appeared out of the blue like this. He hadn't lingered then–because I hadn't given him what he'd wanted–and I would make sure he didn't do so now.

I'd been right about him heading my way when the newspaper article about his accident had come across my feed. He wanted something from me. Again. There was no other reason he showed up. Not for a birthday or graduation from the academy. Not even Christmas.

He rubbed his face. He had a five o'clock shadow that was more salt than pepper. "That's because I'm under a lot of stress." He tipped his head toward the seat across from him. "Sit down. We need to talk."

"No," I said. "We really don't." I lowered the pistol and gritted my teeth. I didn't want this man to be in the same town as me, much less the same house. How dare he tell me to take a seat at my own table. What was it with controlling men?

His familiar brown eyes were filled with a plea. A silent beg. "Meggie, please. My life's in danger. I wouldn't have come if it wasn't desperate."

My stomach clenched, and I worked to steel myself against whatever story he had. His problems weren't mine. They stopped being mine a long time ago.

"I can't help you," I said to forestall whatever favor he was going to ask. This was a familiar dance. He came begging for favors, and I sent him on his way.

He sat there, unmoving, staring at the mouth of his beer and some of my resolve bled away.

Dammit. I hated him, but I couldn't resist his... his... fuck if I knew.

I plopped down in the chair opposite him.

He considered me for a long moment. "You never will forgive me, will you?" He sounded old and tired.

I blew out an impatient breath. "It's not about forgiveness. Although, no–I probably won't. Leaving your daughter to take the fall for your job was pretty low. I spent a year in juvie because of you."

"I keep trying to explain–I had to get out of there or the cops would've picked me up, too. If I'd gone in, I'd still be in jail. I couldn't have helped you from the inside. You were under eighteen." He twisted his beer on the table, watching the condensation drip down its neck. "They go easier on minors. Your record was sealed."

"So you've said." I got it. I did. Logically, it made sense. But emotionally? It had felt like an abandonment. No, it had been just that. I'd been all in with my dad playing cat burglar jewel thief, thinking we were a team except he'd left me to take the fall. A year. In juvie.

What was the saying? *There's no I in team?*

I shook my head, sickened by the sight of him. At what he'd done. What I'd done. The life I had before I returned to Sparks. The one I wanted to forget and tried to put behind me by becoming the good guy. Enforcing the law instead of breaking it.

"So you're desperate." I got back to the point.

"It's Burns. I was working a job for him and got double-crossed by my partner." His eyes went soft. "It should've been you, Meggers."

I slapped my hand on the table. "God, Dad! It will never be me! Never again. I am a *sheriff's deputy*."

He went on like I hadn't interrupted. "My partner took the goods, and I had nothing to give Burns. He's turning the screws on me now—he thinks I'm the double-crosser. I have to do a job to prove my loyalty. I take nothing, the prize is that I get to live." My dad gave me a lopsided smile.

"Burns is your old business partner, right? What is he exactly? A bookie? Loan shark?"

He shook his head. "Worse."

He didn't say more, and I really didn't want to know. I wasn't even sure why I asked in the first place. Any guy who was going to kill my father wasn't someone I wanted to know anything about.

Shit.

"I can't help you, Dad. You know I can't."

He sighed. "Meggie, I can't do it on my own—not with this broken collar bone."

I assumed he got it in that accident I read about.

"I've done all the research and planned it all out. You're the only one who can do it, though."

"You mean there's no one else who will do it for free."

He frowned. "No, it requires a special skill set."

I lifted a brow. "What's that? A sheriff's badge?" I flicked the one on my uniform.

His gaze took in my uniform as if he needed a reminder of the path I'd taken with my life. A *good* one.

"It's your size and agility. It's a skylight job—too

tight... and high for me to get through, even if I wasn't injured."

"Oh no." I huffed out a laugh. "No way. You're out of your mind. Absolutely not." I stood. I needed to get my dad out of my house. This conversation was over. I had nightmares about the last time I crawled through a skylight... and the year that followed.

My dad took the hint and stood. "I need you, Meggie." He spread his hands in supplication. "Burns will kill me if I don't complete this job. I'm in a real pinch here."

"You'll find another way." It was true. My dad was very resourceful. "I'm not getting involved. Never again."

"Meg–"

"Stop calling me that," I snapped. "My name is Megan. I am an officer of the law, not a cat burglar or a jewel thief."

He held his hands out in surrender. "Okay, I'm going. You're right. I'll figure it out."

I fought against the surge of guilt that rose up in me. But no. This wasn't my problem, just like I wasn't his problem when I got picked up and served a year because of him.

He stared at me for a moment then turned toward the door. He looked like nothing but a sad old man with his sagging shoulders and remaining hair that was more gray than brown. I'd once thought he was so powerful. So clever. He'd been my entire world after my mom walked out on us, made all his deals and ventures, his jobs, into a game for me. We were the Dynamic Duo. Batman and Robin although I was more like Batgirl.

I'd blindly done what he'd wanted. Followed orders. Broke the law because that was what my dad had needed me to do. Until it wasn't a game. Wasn't the two of us any longer.

Then it had been just me. Alone. It was safer that way. Juvie had taught a class full of psychological mumbo jumbo to use the time behind bars to distance myself from the old life, the bad influences that had put me in the place. To manifest a future that was bright and sunshiny.

I did just that, not because I believed in rainbows and unicorns but because I couldn't believe or trust anyone but myself. I'd built a future on that. That I was the only one who wasn't going to let me down.

"Take care of yourself," I couldn't stop myself from saying.

He nodded. "Yeah. I'll try. You too, Meg–Megan."

My stomach plummeted the moment he walked out the door. I rubbed the back of my neck.

Nope. Not going to do it. I was definitely not going to feel bad about the stupid shit he got himself into. He'd been in bad spots before, and he'd figure his own way out. I had a job and a life I loved here. I wasn't risking any of it for a guy who had left me out to dry. Who I couldn't trust. No way would I let him control me again.

CHAPTER NINE

HAYES

MEGAN KEPT SETTING the alarm on me. The fact that she thought her security system–a good one–could keep me out was laughable.

It was my sixth night showing up at bedtime, and she made it hard for me to get in every time. Not too hard. Not that I minded. I was glad she was keeping herself safe and that I was the only one getting to her. I wouldn't sleep well if I'd thought otherwise. Not that she wasn't a well-armed, highly trained professional.

I heard her moving around inside. She was home, and she knew I was coming. She had to–I'd been over here like clockwork to service her, as promised.

Still, I didn't knock. Call it male pride or ego or whatever, but I couldn't stand the idea of knocking and waiting to be let in. Especially when the chance of her refusing me entry was always there.

No, this woman needed me to just show up. To prove I was going to keep coming no matter how often she tried to shut me down or set her alarm. She sure as hell loved everything I did once I'd gained entry. I figured she just liked to make me work for it.

And I was willing to do that work.

I unhooked the wire running across her back-door before I slid my lockpick into the doorknob and turned the dials.

When I stepped in, I found myself face to face with the barrel of a Glock 19. I knew my weapons even up close. Megan stood there in her hot-as-fuck pajamas, which consisted of a cropped tank and thin sleep shorts, holding her pistol. My pants instantly got tight, as always happened the moment I saw her, knowing she had nothing on underneath. And her holding a gun?

Fucking hot.

I held up my hands in surrender. "Hey, if you're

not feeling it, just say so, baby doll. I stop when a woman says no." I quirked a smile at her.

She frowned. "Would it kill you to knock?"

Okay, she was in a bad mood but didn't say no. She didn't want me to leave. I could work with that.

"What is it with people breaking into my house these days?"

"*These days?*" I asked sharply, suddenly on full alert. "Did someone else break in?" I tried to remember if the wire I'd pulled had seemed looser than usual.

"*No.*" She said it too quickly.

I'd been trained in interrogation techniques. Interviewing hostiles. All with someone a hell of a lot more difficult. And not in ass-cupping sleep shorts.

Megan was lying to me.

And for some reason, she kept pointing that damn gun at my head.

I arched a brow. "Are you daring me to disarm you, baby doll? Because I had a different kind of tussling in mind tonight, but I am totally down with whatever gets you hot."

Her eyes narrowed, but I saw a gleam of interest in them. She hit the release button to drop the maga-zine cartridge from the Glock then pulled back the slide to spit the live round out onto the floor. She loosened her shoulders. "Show me what you've got, big guy."

Fuck. As much as I loved throwing my weight around in bed with Megan, in this scenario, I was loath to manhandle her. This was a losing proposition.

As in, I'd better let her win because me winning would definitely be the wrong move.

How did I know this? The gun to the head was a pretty solid giveaway.

I eyed her for a solid ten seconds before my hand shot out to knock her wrist up. She landed an impressive karate-style kick in the center of my chest that knocked me back and out of range.

This was how she wanted to play?

"You're toying with me," she accused.

"Nah." I held my hand out for the weapon, and this time she handed it over. When she did, I caught her wrist and spun her around until her back hit my front, and I could restrain her from behind. Our arms were banded about her torso, and my hard dick was nestled against her perfect ass. "I just wait for the right opportunities," I murmured against her ear.

"Mmm." Her body had gone soft and supple

against mine. After six nights, she knew I'd give her everything she needed and more.

"Who broke into your house?" I kept my voice low and seductive like we were still talking about sex.

Wrong move.

She stiffened, further proving she'd lied. "You did," she snapped. "And I'm sick of it. Just ring the damn bell."

I stroked my thumb across the soft skin of her belly. "Give me a damn key."

"Not happening, Hayes." There she went using my call sign again.

I slid my hand up inside her shirt to cup one of her bare breasts, groaning at the feel of that ripe, firm curve in my palm. I dragged my lips along the column of her neck. "Can we take heavy artillery off the table?"

I felt her belly flex in a chuckle and sank my teeth into her neck. She ground that sexy ass of hers back against my lap, making me even harder.

I cupped between her legs and confirmed she wasn't wearing panties under the soft cotton shorts. My fingers found that damp flesh and caressed.

Megan let out a soft sigh.

"That's right, baby doll. I'm going to make you

feel good," I promised, kissing along her neck as I gently worked her folds.

Fine. She didn't want to tell me who broke into her house? I'd figure it the fuck out. I worked for a world-class private security firm and had the persistence of a bulldog. She wasn't the only one who could play detective.

Or, I'd get it out of her eventually. Megan Hager was skittish, that much was sure. But I was in it for the long game. I'd win her over eventually. Earn her trust. Pry her secrets out of her.

Someday, Megan would come to me with her problems, and I would burn the world down to solve them.

I looked forward to that day. In the meantime, I slipped two fingers inside her and made her moan.

CHAPTER
TEN

MEGAN

"DID you finish with the paperwork for the revised parade route?" Mary asked.

I looked up from my work and glanced at Dan. We swiveled in unison toward the office manager who was at her desk by the station's lobby. Fortunately, it was a quiet Saturday, and we hadn't left the station for more than assisting the volunteer fire department with motor vehicle accident training. They'd used a totaled car to practice the jaws of life and other tools that were used on actual scenes. Dan and I led the incident command for it and flagged in a helicopter in a nearby field.

Ford Ledger had purchased–yup, actually bought–a helicopter for the security company he operated. I wasn't exactly sure what he needed a chopper for in rural Montana, but he'd volunteered it, along with the services of the pilot, to the community for emergencies.

Quincy had been quick to introduce herself and work closely with the local paramedics to make a plan if someone needed a flight to the regional hospital in Missoula.

Since then, Dan and I had been planning the route for the annual Labor Day parade. With a bridge under construction, the route had to be shifted this year.

"What's up?" I asked.

Mary pointed to her phone. "That was Mrs. Ledger. She's at the church rummage sale and asking for a ride home."

"No one there can give her a ride?" Dan asked, knowing the event drew in a large crowd.

"Guess not," Mary replied.

Dan checked his watch. "I'll take her. I can stop by Nell's bakery on the way home to pick up little Danny's birthday cake."

Mary shook her head and looked my way. "She specifically asked for Megan."

Dan laughed, and I couldn't miss the mirth in Mary's eyes.

I shook my head and bit my lip to stifle my own smile.

"You've been summoned," Dan murmured.

I stood, and he tossed me the keys to the patrol SUV.

"I assume you told her I was on my way," I said, heading toward Mary and the front of the building.

"Does anyone tell that woman no?" she asked.

"I'll finish the parade route and send it to the mayor," Dan called.

I raised my arm and gave him a little wave over my shoulder. I might report to the sheriff, but everyone in town reported to Mrs. L.

Five minutes later, the spritely old woman slid into the passenger seat, setting her cloth bag on her lap and putting on her seatbelt.

"Thanks so much for collecting me. Ford dropped me off, and I haven't seen him since."

I glanced over my shoulder to check for cars, then headed down the street. "He didn't tell you when he'd be back? That's not like him."

She shrugged. "His mind's distracted these days with Indi and all."

I didn't say anything, only set my blinker and

stopped at an intersection. Ford Ledger distracted? I highly doubted that, even though he was head over heels for Indi. Their love wasn't all calf eyes and pining. It was intense and sharp and deep. The incident with her being kidnapped from her guide trip by a man who'd had her brother killed... it had made their relationship unbreakable.

"What about you, dear?"

"What about me?" I put my foot on the accelerator now that we'd cleared town. The Ledger place was a few miles out.

"I haven't heard about you dating anyone."

I clenched the steering wheel and took a second. If she even scented I had a thing with Hayes, she'd be on it like a bloodhound.

"You would know," I replied.

"Don't sass me, young lady."

I laughed and glanced her way. She was smiling and gave me a wink.

"Is there someone in town wanting to date me?" I asked.

"In town? No. But I do have a number of fine young men staying with me now."

I nodded. "Yes, ma'am. They are fine."

Only a blind woman would disagree; therefore, doing so would make her suspicious.

I slowed and turned down her drive.

"I'm not interested in dating, Mrs. L. I'm content being single." I pulled up in front of her house and put the SUV in park.

"A man's good for a few things. Changing the oil, replacing a furnace filter. A few others. One's good to have around."

I had a feeling she was specifically talking about the *few other* things. I doubted she was referring to talented oral skills or the ability to fuck deep and hard, but that was where my dirty mind went.

"Honey, in this day and age, you don't need to settle down. You're smart. Resourceful. You've got a good job and can take care of yourself."

"Thank you." I wasn't exactly sure where she was going.

"Remember, if all you want is a little sausage, you don't have to buy the whole pig."

She climbed from the car as I choked on a laugh. Turning around, she stuck her head back in the SUV. "Turn this thing off and come inside. You're staying for dinner."

"Are we having sausage?"

She winked. "I'll let you decide."

———

HAYES

I LOVED MRS. L.

Seriously, the woman was something else. She delivered Megan to me for dinner. We weren't alone, but she was here. As we all sat out around the patio table on the back deck, I got to listen to the musical sound of her voice, watch every beautiful expression she made.

Of course, the downside was that apparently, we were pretending we weren't dating. That I didn't know about the birthmark on her left butt cheek or that she liked it best when I took her from behind. Yeah, the deep penetration made her cream *and* scream.

Even knowing all those intimate details about her, not dating her was technically true. She hadn't granted me a date. A movie. Ice cream. Bowling. Whatever people did here in Sparks to get to know each other–outside of bed. But I would think six nights of screamed orgasms would constitute me a peck on the lips or a hand hold or something.

But nope.

She was pretending I was nothing to her.

And my male ego was taking it pretty damned hard.

Especially because Taft and Kennedy kept throwing me smirks like they couldn't believe how...*not far* I'd gotten with this woman. Even Quincy was sending me quizzical looks.

Megan sat next to Quincy, and I plunked down beside her, my plate piled high with Kennedy's barbeque ribs and Mrs. L's corn on the cob, which had just become my new favorite thing. Taft and Kennedy were across from us, Mrs. L on my right.

Ford was in D.C. following up on a lead his–our old–commanding officer had given him. Lincoln had his hands tied when the dishonorable discharge had come down from the top but didn't believe the reason behind it any more than the rest of us. So, he'd been giving Alpha Mountain jobs... and some intel. Hopefully, this one might give all of us a lead on Tully's boss.

I'd tried to drop my hand on Megan's thigh, but she'd moved it off–actually picked up my wrist and shifted my hand to my own lap. Yeah. It was that bad.

"Got any stories about Ford when he was younger?" Quincy asked.

Taft perked up and waved a rib in the air. "Yeah, he's not here. I want to hear about that. Weird girlfriends. Bad haircuts." He thought for a moment. "Mrs. L, please tell me Ford had a mullet."

Mrs. L laughed. "I think I have photos of him with a bowl cut somewhere."

I couldn't help but chuckle at the image of our senior chief with a mullet. He had a good beard going now, but it wasn't the same thing.

"Ford's a few years older than me," Megan said. "I moved away for a while, so I only remember him when he was young. I think we went to the same summer camp."

"Where did you go?" Kennedy asked, and he wasn't wondering about summer camp.

Yeah, I wondered that too. I took a sip of my beer.

Megan reached for the butter and jabbed her knife into the soft spread. As she coated her corn with it, she replied. "Seattle."

"Your parents got jobs there?" Quincy asked.

Megan flicked her a glance and set her knife down after dousing the corn.

"It was just me and my dad, and yes, he got a job. A few actually."

I was thankful my teammates were asking these questions. I wanted to know the answers, but all I was good for was sex. Asking questions outside of if she wanted it harder or deeper was pushing it.

"What brought you back? I mean, you've got to love it here if you gave up Seattle."

"I finished the academy and wanted something quieter than a big city. I always liked it here."

"And your dad?"

Her lips thinned, and she grabbed her tea glass and took a sip. "We're estranged."

"Who wants more potato salad? Get it before the mayonnaise turns," Mrs. L said, picking up the bowl in front of her and passing it to Kennedy. As if she'd ever make something that would poison us.

"I've got a question," I murmured.

She looked to me, those beautiful eyes snagging me. I couldn't miss the wariness, and that meant she didn't want to talk family any longer. So, I steered the conversation to the realm where I knew she'd engage. Happily. Firearms. Maybe I'd actually get a date out of her.

"So, where do the locals go to shoot?" I asked her. Mrs. L could easily answer–Ford, too, if he was here– but I wanted Megan to chime in. "You must have a firing range around here for the law enforcement officials to practice."

Megan quirked a shapely brow at me. "Of course. Why do you ask?"

I shrugged. "Wouldn't mind a little target practice."

Kennedy's brows slammed down, but he took mercy on me and kept his mouth shut. There was no need for her to know that we'd already had target practice two days ago here on the property.

"It's out on Houghton Way." She wiped her mouth with her napkin. "Don't you have your own targets here?"

"Oh, sure," I said with a casual shrug. "But I was thinking about a little friendly competition."

Megan lifted her chin, and her eyes–finally–met mine. "Oh yeah?"

Yup. I had her number.

"Uh huh." I took a pull on the long-neck beer I was nursing. "How do you think your shooting skills rate? Think you could outshoot a SEAL? I mean, the kinds of calls you get out here in Sparks don't require weapons. More like skills with rescuing kittens in a tree."

"That's the fire department," she countered.

"So, you don't even shoot a weapon then. It's all for show."

She considered me as Mrs. L made a funny sound then took a sip of her tea to cover it.

My woman liked to win, I knew that. Which

meant she was assessing her chances before she jumped in. "You don't think I can shoot?"

I shrugged. "It's not a squirt gun in your holster, so I assume you have some skill."

"You're the one with the squirt gun," she murmured.

Everyone heard and laughed. I took it in good stride because while she might be putting down my manhood, it was an acknowledgment that she was familiar with it.

I smiled. I had her right where I wanted her. "Wanna find out what I'm packing?"

Her eyes flared, like the challenge turned her on. "Yeah, I might like that."

Hot, damn. I finally got her to agree to a date.

"Should we make it interesting?" she asked.

God bless every member of my team who kept their mouths shut and looked away. I didn't need anyone telling her I was the team sniper. If she ever bothered to ask more personal questions about me, she might know that by now. But of course, she hadn't.

"What'd you have in mind?"

"Best out of three."

"And the bet?"

"Winner's choice."

Kennedy, who sat across from Megan, rubbed a hand across his mouth to hide his smirk.

I knew they all thought I was going to try to win that bet.

I wasn't. It was Megan's to win. I would lose to her any day of the year. Every day of the year for the rest of my life. If winning made her happy, I'd be the loser. Hands down. No joke.

Because that meant she might get her hands—and mouth—on my squirt gun again.

CHAPTER
ELEVEN

MEGAN

HAVING a key to the local gun range made it easy to practice whenever I wanted. It wasn't like the owner was going to make the sheriff's department staff pay. So, I used my key to unlock the place after hours.

It was just me and Hayes, our weapons and a few boxes of bullets.

The building was on the edge of town, low and squat. Since winter lasted nine months of the year in Sparks, I was used to practicing here. I flicked on the lights and entered the shooting area. "All right Hayes, let's see what you've got."

"Rafael," he corrected, like me calling him Hayes annoyed him.

"Right. Rafael Reyes. What's your middle name?"

He shook his head. "You don't need to know."

Ha. That meant it was something bad. I shouldn't be so curious, but I was. I slipped my hand into his pocket and eased his driver's license out of his wallet without removing it. Being trained as a pickpocket from a young age had few perks.

I held his license up to read aloud, "Rafael Rebel Reyes. *Rebel*? Really?"

"How did you get that?" He tried to snatch the license away, but I stepped back, swinging my hand in the air, away from his reach.

"Triple R's!" I laughed and turned away from him, delighted when he used a martial arts move to whip me around and pin me against the wall, my wrist captured by his large hand. He pried the license from my fingers, his smile warm. "You've got skills, Hager, I'll give you that."

"Oh, now I'm *Hager*?"

He leaned in close and brushed his lips across mine. "Are you going to use my first name?"

"I was thinking I might call you *Rebel*," I teased, snatching his lower lip between my teeth and tugging gently before I released.

He stamped his lips over mine, kissing me until I was breathless. Then he slowly eased back. "Call me *Rebel,* and you're going to experience orgasm denial at a combustion-causing level."

My nipples tingled at the threat. I opened my mouth to test him but closed it again. Orgasm denial didn't sound like my thing.

"Come on, little thief. I want to see you shoot." Hayes sauntered away and stepped into a booth and set his weapon on the high counter in front of him.

His nickname had me stilling, but he meant nothing by it. I shouldn't have stolen his ID. It had been a stupid move that showed off some old skills people didn't need to know about. Including–no especially–Hayes.

"So... winner's choice, right?" I let it go and entered the booth beside him, setting my gun on the counter. With a flick of a switch, the target clip moved toward me. I waited then pinned a paper target to it. Hayes did the same.

"That's right." He leaned against the counter and faced me. Clearly, he wasn't in any rush to shoot. "What's your prize then?" he asked.

I shrugged. What did I want from him?

"Dinner?"

I rolled my eyes. "We're not dating, Hayes."

"Fine, not dinner. I'll clean all your windows."

"Not dating," I said again.

"I have to do a hundred push-ups?"

I raked my gaze down his toned body. He was in jeans and a snug black t-shirt that only amplified the size of his pecs and biceps. "Somehow I don't think that's much of a hardship for you."

He winked. "Okay, then I'll... detail your car."

"Not–"

"Dating," he finished. "All you want me for is my dick?"

The way he asked, he should have been asking in jest, but I could tell that it perhaps bothered him. I'd made it clear, *very* clear, that I didn't want more. He'd gone along with it, but he kept coming back, like a bad rash.

"And other things." I pulled my mouth to the side and studied him. "You're skilled with your hands. That tongue of yours should be registered as a weapon."

He couldn't help but grin. "Anytime, baby doll. You can have it or any part of me."

I loved that he was so open, so generous. Yes, sexually, but he seemed to be enmeshed in the group that made up Alpha Mountain Security. He wasn't a loner like me. Which made me think of my dad and his little visit and fortified my walls against letting him in.

"My nana told me I'm very generous."

"I'm pretty sure your grandmother wasn't talking about the number of orgasms you give a woman."

He shrugged, unashamed.

"She had eight children," he commented, scratching his jaw with a finger that had been inside me. "I'm sure my *abuelo* took good care of her."

I widened my eyes at the fact that he was talking about his grandparents' sex life. Then laughed.

"What? I have a very close family."

"And big, if she had eight kids."

He nodded. "I have twenty-two first cousins. Sunday dinner can get pretty crazy."

"I assume they're not here in Sparks."

He shook his head. "Albuquerque."

"Then why aren't you there? I mean, you left the Navy, so why not go home to be with your well-sexed nana?"

He hesitated, and I sensed a story.

I set my weapon down and turned to fully face him.

"My cousins are entrepreneurial... and their

business ventures aren't exactly legit, if you catch my drift."

My lips parted in surprise at this reveal. Hayes had criminals in his family, too. But he wasn't one himself.

"My parents were afraid I'd get pulled into it, so they convinced me to join the Navy straight out of high school."

"Wow. Unexpected." Who knew Hayes and I had this in common?

He shrugged. "It was a fork in the road moment, you know? I rebelled against the future they were offering me."

"So, you *are* a rebel," I teased. "Rebel with a cause."

His lips twisted in a grin. "I guess. My whole life could've gone one way, toward a life in the production and sales of narcotics, but because I walked away from family, it went in a completely different direction. That decision salvaged my soul. I still have honor. I can walk into a church or a school and hold my head up high. I can fuck a sheriff's deputy." He winked, and I rolled my eyes.

For one moment there, I'd considered telling him I understood. That I had unpleasant characters in my family line as well. But my honor hadn't been salvaged. I didn't take the right fork in the road. Sure, I had after juvie, but the stain was still there on my soul. The possibility of getting sucked back in or having everyone find out always loomed as a potential disaster.

"So, were they mad? Your cousins?" I asked.

"Yeah. They still want me involved–even more now with the skills I have. That's why I can't really go back. I love my family, and I miss the hell out of them, but I didn't even tell them I was out of the service. Only my parents and grandmother know."

"I'm sorry."

He shrugged. "It's fine. The team's my family now. Do you remember Buck? Indi's brother."

"Of course. He worked at his parents' hardware store. I used to go in and get popcorn, and he'd be there, sorting nails and bolts. Looking back, he'd probably been in trouble, and they gave him ridiculous busy work as punishment."

The smile he gave me was slow and sad, and I knew he was thinking of his friend who'd been killed in Afghanistan.

"That sounds like him. Unlike Ford, Buck was the easygoing one. A team is tight. Closer than a family in ways because we trust each other with our lives."

He picked up a bullet and fiddled with it as he continued.

"When Buck died and then Ford got kicked out, it was tough. I was the first one Ford called when he started his business. I didn't re-up because I wanted to stay with my men."

Wow. He was so flipping honorable and supportive. Then I processed that Ford had been *kicked out.* I hadn't heard that before, which meant even Mrs. L wanted it to remain a secret.

I wasn't the only one with skeletons in my closet.

"You have two families. You're doubly lucky," I replied.

Yeah, it stung. I saw the way Indi was with her parents. How Ford was with Mrs. L. Dan and his wife with their kids. Families who were there for each other and not to help with grand theft.

"You said your mom left," he commented.

I didn't usually answer questions about my mom, but for some reason, it felt natural with Hayes. I'd been pushing him away, but he was actually very easy to talk to.

I nodded. "When I was eight. She just up and left. My dad said she always had men courting her. Even as a married woman. He figured she used her best qualities to generate a more tempting offer than small-town Montana living."

"What are those?" he asked.

I swirled my finger in a circle in front of my face. "Her looks. Miss Montana 1985. She knew how to work it." I sighed. "I remember how men would rush to help her everywhere we went. The grocer would carry her bags out. She never opened her own door."

"So now you won't let a man help," Hayes said, softly enough that it didn't goad me.

I picked my weapon back up. "I don't want to depend on anyone."

"Yeah, I get that, but having people you can trust doesn't make you weak." He shot me a wry smile. "Neither does being beautiful."

His dark eyes roved over my face as I spoke.

"Yeah, I look just like her."

"She's a mighty pretty woman then," he said. "But she doesn't sound like she has your character."

I blinked. "What?"

He pushed off the counter, set the bullet down and came close, tipping my chin up. "A person's character gives them depth. Makes them worthy."

"I thought that was honor," I replied, suddenly feeling a touch vulnerable.

"Same thing."

I shook my head and stepped back. I didn't want his praise because he was so very wrong.

"It's not the same thing at all," I said.

This conversation was heavy. Way too heavy to have with a guy I was using for sex.

"You asked what I want if I win?" I turned and grabbed my safety goggles.

He stepped back to his booth. "Yeah?"

"Control." I pushed the button, and my paper target zipped back to the farthest distance in the range. "You'll give me control when we fuck later."

Because it seemed that was the only thing I could handle right about now. My father was out there. I'd turned him away, but he wouldn't be gone forever. I couldn't control him. I never could. My mother left, and I'd been helpless to stop her. To be enough for her to even think about staying.

And Hayes? He couldn't be more than a fling. He was honorable in everything he'd mentioned. He wouldn't want me if he knew the truth of my past. Of what I'd done. Of the father who'd returned to pull me back into the life.

All I could be for him was a good time.

That was all I deserved. But I could get it on my terms. Tie him to the damned headboard and finally have a man under my thumb.

I smiled and tucked my hearing protection into my ears.

"That's what I want," I called, then raised my arms in front of me. Aimed. Shot.

Over the loud burst of gunfire, I heard him say, "Yes, ma'am."

CHAPTER TWELVE

MEGAN

AS IT TURNED OUT, controlling Hayes in bed last night had been just as fun as having him take charge.

I strongly suspected he'd let me win, but he had allowed me to handcuff him to the bedpost and tease him with my mouth and hands until I thought he'd tear the bed apart to get on top of me. Only then did I climb over him and ride to my heart's content.

I'd loved it, but I suspected there would be retribution tonight, and I had to say, I was looking forward to it. Hayes in charge was a beautiful thing to receive.

Damn, the guy was definitely growing on me, despite my effort to keep it as casual as it could possibly be. There was nothing about him I didn't like. He pushed but respected. Was steadfast in his pursuit of me but honored all my boundaries.

Basically, he was a stand-up guy.

Part of me almost wanted to grant him that date.

Almost.

I smiled to myself when I heard a car pull up outside. Here he was, right on schedule.

Except the heavy knock at the door didn't sound like him. For one thing, he didn't knock. He disarmed my security system without knowing the passcode. If he did knock, it certainly wouldn't be in that loud, impatient way.

Frowning, I yanked on a pair of jeans and palmed my Glock while someone nearly broke my door down.

I rode the edge of pissed off as I threw open the door. The moment I did, three guys pushed past me into the room. I stumbled back and left the door wide open.

"Well, well. You turned out as pretty as your mom, didn't you?"

"Who the hell are you?" I snarled although I had a pretty good idea.

"Your daddy didn't mention me? He mentioned you. I'm your new friend Burns."

Just as I'd thought. *Fuck.*

He had the nerve to reach out and caress a lock of my hair. I pegged him in his early forties, younger than my dad. He was dressed in a suit with a black t-shirt beneath the jacket. His goons were a little more casual, but none of them blended into Sparks. Then again, this wasn't their turf. It was mine, which meant he *really* wanted to talk with me.

I yanked my head back. My stomach turned at the scent of stale cigarette smoke.

"I'm surprised you don't remember me. The Empress sapphire ring?"

Old memories soured my stomach more than him.

He'd been part of the Empress sapphire job, the guy with the contacts to move the stolen goods. I'd never met him as a kid but knew he was a dealer in art, jewels, weapons, and pretty much anything else that could be traded on the black market. He was the guy who financed big jobs, which was, I assumed, how my dad ended up being his grunt. The cord would never be cut between them.

Burns eyed the revolver in my grip. I took in their

weapons. All of the men packed heat. It was like a western standoff, and I was losing.

Three against one were shitty odds.

If I meant to shoot my gun, I should've done it before now. I'd already blown my window of opportunity, dammit. Killing a man–or men–protecting my own home was legal. I was also a law enforcement officer being threatened.

The bastard had the nerve to hold out his hand, palm up. Smiled.

I didn't move, weighing my options. Which, frankly, were shit.

If he'd wanted me dead, that would have happened by now too.

"What do you want?"

"For starters, your gun. Give it to me, little girl." His tongue flicked out and licked his lower lip.

Little. Girl?

Little fucking girl?

I was pretty sure literal steam came out of my ears.

But then Burns jerked his chin at the bigger guy with him, who held up his phone screen, and ice-cold washed across my skin. I blinked, trying to figure out what I was seeing. It was a live feed of my dad, tied to a chair in what looked like a warehouse.

He'd been beaten and had a gag shoved in his mouth.

Fuck.

I wanted to puke for what my dad's life had become. How Burns had such ruthless control over him. And now me.

I only hesitated a moment longer before I placed my Glock in his palm.

"That's better. We're just here to talk, Meg. We didn't come to hurt you although Jake does have a thing for torturing women." He tipped his head at the skinnier of the two men with him. The one with a gold tooth and tattoos across his knuckles, which he actually cracked now for full cinematic effect.

I didn't say anything. If he expected me to beg and plead for my dad's or my own life, it wasn't happening. That didn't mean I wasn't a little afraid and a hell of a lot pissed on the inside. I tipped my chin up.

"What do you want?" I repeated my earlier question.

Burns strode to my sofa and made himself at home, settling in and crossing his ankle over a knee. He even had the audacity to set his arms wide along the back. His goons remained standing. "Have a seat,

Meg." He indicated the armchair across from him as if this was his house, not mine.

Before I could even decide whether to comply or not, the goons grabbed my arms and propelled me to the chair, where they shoved me down.

My upper lip curled with rage, but I kept my mouth shut.

Burns looked the same as I remembered. Not good-looking but distinguished with graying hair and a lined face from what I guessed was years of smoking. "I understand your dad already paid you a visit. Is that right?"

I gave a single nod even though I was sure he knew the answer already.

"He needs your help with a job."

I gazed sullenly at the man. If he expected me to make conversation, he was going to be disappointed.

"He said you told him no."

"Uh-huh."

Burns held my gun in his lap and removed the ammo from it with an ease that proved he knew his way around a weapon. "You see, that doesn't work for me, Meg. Your dad owes me money. A lot of it. And I need him to complete this job, so I can be made whole. Do you understand?"

Was it childish that I didn't feel like saying *yes*?

Burns lifted his chin at the guy with the phone again.

"Hit him," the goon ordered.

He turned the screen to my face to witness someone punch my dad's jaw. The sound of bone hitting bone and my dad's resulting groan sickened me.

"Yes! I understand!" I shouted. I didn't like my father. He'd made shitty choices I hadn't recognized when I was a kid that were just... wrong. I hadn't understood then as that was what I'd thought parent/child relationships were. Looking back, it was really, really whack.

He'd left me when I'd been caught by the police, not even visiting me in juvie. He'd been on the run, and his neck had been more important to him than his own daughter.

It seemed that was still the case since Burns was sitting on my sofa threatening me.

Using whatever shred of love I had for my father against me.

I hated him. Hated myself for caring because all it did was show how weak I was. How easy I was to manipulate and control. Still.

"Good." Burns looked satisfied. "So. Here's what's

going to happen. You're going to complete the job for him, and then I'll let him live. Deal?"

Oh no.

Fuck no.

My throat closed like someone was choking the life out of me.

"I can't," I managed to say. "I'm in law enforcement. My job is to arrest people who do exactly what you're expecting me to do."

Someone struck my dad again.

My stomach roiled.

"Besides it being illegal, I don't even know what the job is," I continued. "He didn't tell me anything about it. I'm not in this line of work anymore."

Burns gave me a faint smile. "It's not a line of work one ever leaves, little girl. Once you're in our world, you stay. You got caught and paid the price. You're a criminal. This life, it's where you belong. Since you'll probably lose your job, I'll give you one. You're talented. Pretty. A convicted felon. Everything I'm looking for in employees."

I definitely wanted to argue that point but was smart enough to keep my mouth shut this time.

Burns reached into the pocket of his jacket and pulled out an envelope. On the outside was my name written in my dad's hectic writing. "Your dad was kind enough to outline the plans for you. You have one week to get it done or your dad dies. Understand?"

An out-of-body feeling came over me. It was the same one I'd had that night the police picked me up with the Empress sapphire. My eyes glazed over. I withdrew. Separating the real me from what was going on.

Faintly, I found myself nodding my agreement because while my dad had sat at my kitchen table and told me they were going to kill him if he didn't do a job, it wasn't the same thing as this. As Burns having my father beaten on command. On giving his life a timeframe.

On giving me the sole role of saving him.

One week to steal something worth killing for.

All by myself.

For a man who might be my father but with whom I had zero relationship.

I should just say no. Or call in the feds to deal with this.

I was a sheriff's deputy. I had connections. Resources to help me.

Except they wouldn't care about my dad's life. They wouldn't make sure he got out alive.

As much as I wanted to believe I didn't care

either, it wasn't true. I may hold a grudge against my dad and put as much distance between us as possible, but wanting him dead was something different altogether. I didn't want to love my father, but deep down, beneath the anger, I did. He was the only family I had, and I couldn't live with knowing he'd died because I didn't help.

Because I could.

Dammit.

"Good. Steal the Skard blade, and we'll be in touch to make the trade. The seax for your dad's life." Burns stood and pocketed my ammo, setting the Glock on the sofa cushion.

I didn't know what he was talking about, what a seax was, but I knew the details were in the envelope.

I pushed to my feet. Burns walked up to me and got a little too close. I refused to step back, to let him know he got to me. He stared down at me with a little smile laying around his lips. "It's good to have you back on the team, Meg."

My brain revolted at his words, but I was careful to show nothing. I didn't answer, just waited until he moved toward the door. The two goons flanked me until he'd reached it, then they followed.

I didn't know how long I stood there without

moving or breathing. Maybe only a few seconds. Maybe it was minutes.

All I knew was that when I heard the sound of footsteps out front, I wanted to hide rather than face the man who made them.

CHAPTER
THIRTEEN

HAYES

"MEGAN?" I tapped the unlatched door and pushed it open.

I'd sat across the street watching three guys walk out of her house. Three guys who didn't look like they belonged anywhere in Sparks, Montana. In fact, they didn't seem to belong in the state or the region, for that matter. They looked metropolitan. Criminal. Very dangerous.

More than a little out of place in my woman's house.

"Not tonight, Hayes." Megan's voice sounded broken. Tired. A little shaky.

I stomped in to find her snatching a gun from the sofa in her living room.

"I said, *not tonight*," she snapped, without turning.

"Okay." I forced myself to make my voice soft as I approached her. Something was wrong. Very, very wrong. And those guys had everything to do with it.

Had they hurt her? Touched her?

Megan didn't like to share much with me. Getting personal had been an ongoing battle, so she probably wasn't going to tell me what was going on. But there was no way I was going to walk away from her place and leave her to spend the night alone. Not with those guys out there.

"Hey," I said softly, touching her waist like she wasn't holding a gun. "Are you okay?"

She worked to swallow and failed. She couldn't even look me in the eye.

"Scratch that," I said. Megan was skittish, like a mare ready to bolt at the slightest thing. "May I hold you?"

She drew in a sharp breath as I slowly tugged her against my body. After a moment, she exhaled and rested her forehead on my shoulder.

"I didn't like the looks of those guys, baby doll."

She sucked in another ragged breath, held it, and

released it slowly. Her body was still and taut as a bowstring ready to be plucked. She held her gun, so no way was I setting her off.

"You don't have to tell me what's going on, but I'm not leaving you tonight. There's just no fucking way I'm walking out that door."

"Hayes." Her voice sounded strangled like she was trying to keep from crying.

I cupped her nape and kissed the top of her head. "I'm not leaving," I said in my most stubborn tone. I may have let her set a million boundaries to keep distance between us, but if she tried to send me away, I'd have to say no.

She pulled away and walked toward the bedroom. The pistol was still in her hand, and her shoulders sagged. I followed behind, a deep furrow between my brows.

Whatever was going on with her went so much deeper than I'd imagined. I'd thought she had relationship issues. Maybe a crappy ex-boyfriend had fucked her over. Made her think having no relationship was better than being in a shitty one. But this was different. Really fucking different, and I recognized it not because I was a man, but because I was a soldier. I knew bad shit. I'd seen it. Fought it. And she had active trouble. Criminal trouble, by the looks of it, and I strongly suspected her life was in danger.

She didn't turn the light on when she got to the bedroom, but she did strip out of her clothes. I stood there, watching in the dim light, trying to figure out what the fuck to do.

The men were gone. For now. I'd ensure her security system was online. She had her weapon. She had me. She was safe.

But for how long? What was she involved in? How could I solve it? To make all her problems go away?

I needed to get Kennedy to pull the feed from her security system and run the faces of those assholes. And run the plate number I'd memorized.

As soon as Megan finished stripping, she came to me and unbuckled my belt. I hissed when her knuckles brushed over my lower belly on their way south.

"No talking," she murmured, grasping my dick in her small hand. She pumped it once, and she was gifted with a spurt of pre-cum.

Okay. Fine.

This was what she needed?

Yeah, okay. I'd give it to her. I'd *always* give her that. Nothing could stop me from satisfying my woman. I wasn't sure if she was doing this to distract herself or to distract me.

In this moment, it didn't matter. She was turning to me. Staying with me. Finding solace or distraction in my body.

I'd fuck her until she forgot all her problems. As her man, that was my job. But it was also to protect her and take care of anything that kept her from smiling. Later, I'd text Kennedy and check the perimeter. And Megan wasn't leaving my sight until I had this shit figured out. Whether we were naked was up to her.

CHAPTER
FOURTEEN

MEGAN

AFTER SEX, I kicked Hayes out. He talked a good game about staying the night, but after I told him not to talk, I'd dropped to my knees. I figured he couldn't ask any questions if he was too focused on his dick in my mouth. I certainly couldn't answer any. When I'd swallowed the last drop of his release, he'd lifted me and tossed me onto the bed, returning the favor.

He hadn't wanted to leave, but there was no way in hell I was doing pillow talk. He'd given in, but I could tell he hadn't been happy.

Too bad. I wasn't happy either. He'd seen Burns and his men. He was smart, but a preschooler could tell they didn't belong in Sparks. I didn't want him knowing anything about this, about Burns or my dad or what I was up against.

Hayes was a Navy SEAL–he fought for his country. Served for the freedom of others. He had honor and deserved respect. I may be serving my community now, but it was because I was repaying a debt to society. I always knew my past might jump up and bite me in the ass, and it seemed that tonight it had. So, keeping my distance from Hayes was no longer just an inclination–it was a full-blown need.

I didn't want him to know about my past. I didn't want it to cloud his opinion of me. I especially didn't want him to get sullied by me if things blew up.

He deserved someone better than me, someone without my baggage. Because I had a lot of it, and it was getting heavier. With a stupid Viking dagger.

After I kicked him out, I reloaded my pistol and opened the envelope Burn had left me.

It was all the details about the theft. The target acquisition was a Viking weapon, circa 970 A.D. named the Alfson seax, after its original seller, a mid-nineteenth century Dutch collector. Pictures of it on the Internet showed a bone grip with etched Norse knotwork studded with rubies, sapphires, and diamonds. It was believed to have originally been owned by a nobleman of some kind.

The piece was stolen by Nazi looters during World War II, only to resurface from an anonymous seller at a famous auction house last month.

The buyer, Hollywood movie star Lucas Straight, was the highest bidder for the Alfson Seax which completed his collection of Viking artifacts, normally kept on display at his Montana property. A second home to escape the insanity of LA. Since this was the *pièce de résistance*, his entire collection would be lent to the Smithsonian for the month of September, and armed transport had been arranged in just over a week.

Hence, the window of opportunity.

My dad had the building plans for the guy's house from the county planning office, as well as a hand-sketched layout of the glass display case. Yeah, it was weird for a place in Bumfuck, Montana to have art displayed so grandly. It even featured wired security, and the room had laser crisscrossing the floors. No windows, only one door, but there was a small skylight. All of that for one rich man's obsession with the Vikings.

Which was where I came in. To snag the dagger from the tricky location. The skylight would've been too difficult for a man my dad's size to navigate. Even the roof was too steep and dangerous at his age. Yeah, I could see why he'd wanted my help for this job.

No, it wasn't *help*. He'd wanted me to do it for him. The only way he could assist out in the middle of nowhere was be a getaway driver, and that wasn't really necessary because being so far out of any town, there wasn't anyone to get away from.

Ugh. So annoying. I could do it. The job was hard but not impossible.

I sat at my computer and researched it all. While my dad was good at stealing, I didn't trust him. A job had been fucked up before, and I'd paid the price because I'd let him blindly guide me.

It just went against everything I now stood for. Like abiding by the law. And not contributing to the delinquency of my father. I'd spent all that time in juvie vowing to myself I wouldn't go back. That I'd find a better life that stayed on the right side of right and wrong.

But his life–and mine–were on the line. Hard to see how I had any choice here. I could go to jail. Lose my job. Be shunned by the town that embraced me. My life would be over–again–because of my dad.

Of choices I hadn't made back in the day, but I was making now.

Hayes would think horrible things about me, exactly as I expected. He'd know I'd been right to give him nothing more than my body.

I hadn't committed a crime beyond breaking the speed limit since I walked out of juvie. I swore I'd never go back or get sucked into the life.

Until now.

CHAPTER
FIFTEEN

HAYES

"HERE'S WHAT I KNOW."

Kennedy spun in his desk chair as I came in the command room. I'd been up his ass from the moment he stirred at sunrise to research Megan's intruders.

Now it was only eight, but the scent of garlic and meatballs from the kitchen made my stomach rumble. Mrs. L said she was making Italian for dinner, and it seemed to be an all-day process.

I'd already done five miles with Taft then showered. Kennedy had kicked me out after I'd shared all the details I could about the men at Megan's house.

Now, I dropped into Mrs. L's old chair. It had lace doilies on the armrests and a basket of yarn sat beside it. I felt out of place in the thing but had to admit it was comfortable.

"Her security system's good. Too good for a small-town deputy," he said.

"I noticed." After almost a week of shutting it down, I knew it thoroughly. "Close to what we installed for Indi."

He nodded.

"I was able to tap into her feeds and got images of the men," he said.

"The guy in the suit. He's the one I want to know about," I told him.

He nodded again and pulled the lollipop from his mouth. Roscoe trotted in from the kitchen and nudged my thigh for a pet. I obliged, and he plopped onto his butt and leaned in, expecting me to keep at it.

"Gabriel Burns. His wrap sheet's a mile long. Based out of Spokane."

"That's a few hours away," I commented.

"A long way to go to chat up a specific woman."

"Go on." I knew there was more. A long list of priors would have plenty to talk about.

"Loan shark. High-end broker of black-market

ALPHA MOUNTAIN: REBEL   143

goods–like stolen art, jewels, endangered animals, etc. He's got a few legit businesses in the city and plenty of under-the-table ones."

A guy like that chatting up a twenty-something woman? "Why's he visiting Megan? A crook and a deputy. Not the perfect match."

He pointed at me and turned to his monitor. Pushed a few buttons. "No idea, so I did a search on your girlfriend."

She wasn't a girlfriend because she was still kicking me out of her bed every night. But Megan didn't turn down sex. Hell, she'd initiated it the night before, even dropped to her knees for me and–

Fuck.

Then she'd tossed my clothes at me like every other night, even though I'd told her I was staying. It was her eagerness to have me gone that left me worried. She'd been scared last night. Upset. She tried to hide it and refused to talk about it, but I could tell. If she wanted me out of there so badly– more so than other nights–then she was keeping something from me. Something big. Which meant I needed answers, and they weren't coming from her.

I left so I could get answers, not to do as she'd said.

I got Kennedy involved because *my woman* was

going solo on something that involved a big shot bad guy from out of state.

"Megan Ann Hager. Twenty-nine. Born here in Sparks to Patricia Spitz Hager and Colin Hager. Mom got a Florida driver's license when Megan was eight, so I assume that's when she bolted. Check out her DL photo." He pointed to an image he pulled up.

"Shit, she's beautiful," I commented on the older photo. I saw Megan in her mom. A lot. Same dark hair, eyes. Full lips, high cheekbones.

"Yeah. Dad's been arrested for some petty crimes. Pickpocketing. Burglary. Trespassing."

"In Sparks?"

"London. Rome. One in Seattle. No steady paychecks. Hasn't filed a tax return since he left Sparks."

"Sounds like a winner," I mutter. "Probably has a lot more jobs under his belt than the ones he got arrested for. The other day, Megan stole my ID right out of my wallet in my pocket. I wouldn't tell her my middle name."

Kennedy smiled. "Is that so, Rafael Rebel?"

"I didn't think of it at the time, but now I'm guessing she has a particular skill set. Maybe Daddy taught her a few things besides how to ride a bike and parallel park."

"No record of a high school graduation for Megan, but records show she got her GED."

"Why would she get a GED? That means she either ditched high school, never went... or something else."

"Went to the police academy, so she needed it for that. Then moved here. Alone."

I scratched Roscoe's ear, and he groaned in satisfaction, his eyes falling closed.

"Let me check on something." He turned to his monitor and typed faster than a steno pool loaded with caffeine. "GED was issued in a suburb of Seattle."

"She said she was estranged from her dad. No photos in her house of either of her parents," I shared.

He turned to face me again. "Mrs. L said her mom's been long gone since she was a kid. As for her dad, my spidey sense tells me I don't like him."

"That's good enough for me."

"Maybe she's trouble, too."

"No," I snarled immediately.

Kennedy lifted his gaze to mine and held it.

I shook my head. "She's not." I searched for something that proved it but couldn't come up with anything other than my own spidey sense. Megan was a good person. I was sure of it.

"If she's not letting you in, maybe she's not the one."

I didn't like his statement but appreciated the honesty. "She lets me in her bed, but it's pretty obvious she's hiding something. Add that Burns fucker into the mix, and there are definitely secrets. I don't think she's keeping them from me specifically. I think she's keeping them from everyone."

"The fact that you're a Navy SEAL makes it a hell of a lot harder to keep secrets."

She was scared last night. That much I was sure of. It proved something, didn't it? It proved she wasn't in with a man like Burns. She was afraid of him.

"She's alone, and I think in way over her head," I said.

Kennedy turned back to the screen. "I was able to pull her search history from her browser at home."

I should have been pissed he invaded her privacy, but sometimes you had to do the wrong thing to protect what was right.

"She was up researching a couple things last

night after you left. I presume it was after you left, or else you're a real dud in bed."

I glared. "Shut up, asshole. What did she research?"

"She read up on a certain Viking weapon called the Alfson seax."

"What the hell's a seax?" I asked.

"A dagger. A big, fancy, old knife with jewels and gold and stuff. It was just sold at auction to Lucas Straight."

"The actor?"

He nodded. "Yeah. And guess where he's keeping it?"

"Just tell me, fuckface."

Kennedy had the nerve to pause for dramatic effect. I swore for a serious badass SEAL, he was such a girl. "At his second home, about ninety minutes from here. Straight spends his summers playing cowboy."

I whistled. "Whoa. Okay. What else?"

"Her other search was for Lucas Straight plus Conifer, Montana."

"Okay, so...she's what? Planning on stealing this thing? Is that what we're thinking?"

I wouldn't have pegged Megan for a thief. Ever.

Kennedy shrugged. "Either that, or she's on his security detail. But somehow I don't think Gabriel Burns is Straight's hiring manager."

Fuck. I scrubbed a hand across my face then pulled up my phone. Last night I'd been dastardly enough to install a tracking app on Megan's phone when she'd used the bathroom. If she didn't notice it and kept her location service on, I'd be able to keep tabs on her.

Again, totally breaking privacy laws, but I didn't give a shit.

"Maybe it's her dad who's doing the job, and she's going to arrest him," I offered up another option.

"Maybe, but why would Burns show up at her house? Why would a guy like him go to a law enforcement officer? It makes no sense."

I didn't like where he was going. I pulled up the app for tracking Megan's cell and–

Bingo! I found her. Fuck. Driving out of town in the direction of Conifer.

I held up my phone, and his eyebrows winged up.

"Text me the address for Lucas Straight's place?" I asked.

"She's headed there? This doesn't look good."

I glared, and he raised his hands.

"Sure." He spun back to his wall of monitors. "What are you going to do now?"

"Follow her."

CHAPTER
SIXTEEN

MEGAN

I PULLED down a long drive to Lucas Straight's vacation home about ninety minutes from Sparks. Considering how much money the guy was supposed to have, the place wasn't as fancy as I expected. I guessed he had about twenty acres and a house with four or five bedrooms. It was the river that ran through the land that made the place valuable. I guessed he was a fisherman as much as a Viking lover and wanted better water access than a state-of-the-art kitchen.

That boded well for me, but I didn't guess when it came to a job. Expect the unexpected, my father always said. While he wasn't a Boy Scout, he also used their motto, always be prepared.

That was why I was here. I glanced around, took in the two-story farmhouse to validate everything my dad had shared. Security cameras in the eaves aimed at the front door. I'd recognized sensors as I turned onto the driveway. If someone was home, he or she knew I was here.

I parked my older Subaru far enough away where the license plate couldn't be seen by cameras, slid on a pair of fake tinted glasses, fluffed the red-haired wig I'd put on beneath a cowgirl hat, and made my way to the front door. I rang the bell and took in the door. Solid wood. Deadbolt. Sensor in the top right corner. The windows that flanked it were new. Double pane. Closed even though it was eighty degrees out.

A woman came to the door wiping her hands on a dishtowel. Fifties. Not from around here based on the stylish cut of her hair and the designer brand on her jeans.

"Hi. I'm Lacey, and I'm here for the interview." I smiled, trying to appear as benign as possible as I took in everything beyond the woman inside the house.

The woman frowned. "Interview?"

"For the farrier job," I replied. Over her shoulder, I took in the entry, the stairs rising directly behind her with a hall beside that led, I assumed, to the kitchen. On one side of her was a den, the other a living room. They were simply furnished but professionally styled as if out of a magazine. Artwork hung on the walls. Even a tapestry by the fireplace.

"I'm sorry, I don't even know what that is."

I laughed, waved it off. "No one does. I'm a horse shoe-er." I glanced left and right, pretending to be lost and scoped out the other security on the front. "I am at the right place, aren't I? This is the Chalmers spread."

The woman looked relieved at my words. "The Chalmers? I think they're the next ranch down. Maybe the one after that. I'm only here a few weeks in the summer, so I haven't met them yet."

I closed my eyes for a second and tried to look sheepish. "Gah. Sorry! The land starts to look the same, and it's not like there are house numbers this far out."

She laughed with me. "No worries."

I stepped back, gave a little wave and headed back to my car. I heard the door close, and I took one last moment to look around.

No trees by the house. No shrubs or plantings to

ALPHA MOUNTAIN: REBEL   153

hide behind. No pets, inside or out. One driveway in and out, unless accessed by foot. The roof was as steep as my father had pointed out, and I could see a few skylights up there. Newer ones, so they were surely wired.

The woman didn't seem like someone who'd just bought a five million-dollar Viking dagger, but I had to assume her husband, the movie star, had the hobby.

I pulled back onto the road and headed toward Sparks. I had more studying to do and had to come back for recon, but at least I had a solid house layout and a personal visual of the roof. A plan was coming together for a nighttime break-in. I had to identify when the Straights would be out of the house. I also had to figure out what to do about my bedmate. Sex was great and all, but Hayes was going to be a cock-blocker for my robbery.

I drove around the curve of the long private drive and hit the brake.

There, blocking my access to the road, stood a truck.

A truck I recognized all too well.

Hayes had followed me. The asshole!

I gunned the car like I was going to crash into the side of the truck, only stopping at the last possible minute, my tires sliding on the crushed gravel, almost close enough to touch the paint of his truck.

Yeah, I was driving getaway cars before I was out of middle school. I had not lost any high-speed chases since I'd joined the sheriff's department. I definitely knew how to handle a vehicle.

Of course, Hayes, the bastard, didn't even flinch. He just sat in the front seat of that truck watching me. Waiting.

I threw open my door and climbed halfway out of the car, gesturing impatiently. "Get out of the middle of the road!"

Hayes rolled the passenger side window down and shook his head. He looked sexy as hell in a base-ball cap–he had yet to adopt the cowboy hats more commonly worn in Montana–and a t-shirt that stretched around his bulky muscles. "Not until you tell me what's going on. Why the fuck you're wearing a wig."

"*Hayes. Move.* You have no idea what you're interfering with."

"So tell me."

I looked around as if someone could see us. "I can't. It's police business. Now move it, or I'll arrest you for obstruction of justice." It was a sad day for me when I started using my job to cover my tracks, but hey–a girl had to do what a girl had to do.

He tilted his sunglasses down. "Uh huh. So... this doesn't have anything to do with stealing a Viking dagger to sell to Gabriel Burns?"

My stomach dropped like a brick to my feet. I wanted to both puke and cry at the same time. Knowing Hayes was aware of the worst of me hurt more than anything Burns had done to scare and manipulate me last night.

I sat there stunned, having no idea what to say. All I could do was blink, flush furiously and try to come up with a lie. Instead, I asked the truth.

"How... how do you know about that?"

He gave me a pointed look. "Baby doll, don't insult me. I saw those men leaving your house, and you think I'd leave it alone. We tapped into your security feed."

Of course he did.

"We?"

"We. My team. All of us at Alpha Mountain."

"You watch my security feed." I didn't state it as a question.

"When I want answers you won't give me. That involves your safety. Come on," he said, tipping his head. "Follow me to the end of this road and pull over. We need to talk."

Waves of both clammy panic and itchy heat swam down my midsection. I felt as caught as I had that night the police picked me up in Seattle with the Empress ring on my finger. Frozen and blank. All I could do was nod and get back in my car. Follow Hayes a mile down the road where he parked under a tree.

He got out and opened my door. "Get out."

Numbly, I removed my seat belt and obeyed.

He fingered the red wig. "Red, huh?"

I couldn't seem to answer him. I couldn't even swallow down the lump in my throat. He put his hand at my lower back and guided me to his truck. "Climb in, baby doll."

In the back of my mind, I considered my options. Bolting. Fighting. They were all absurd, but even if they'd been viable, I wouldn't. It was Hayes. I owed him whatever it was he was about to demand. Not because we were in a relationship. Not because we'd had sex a few times. But because he was a good man. I respected him.

I wanted to still be that person he thought I was. At least for a little bit longer before he bolted. Or turned me in. Or both.

I made my fingers work to open the door to his truck, and I slid into the passenger side. He shut the door after me, and I couldn't bring myself to look at him.

When he climbed behind the wheel, he didn't start up the truck. Instead, he sat there, like he was gathering his thoughts, looking out the front windshield.

"So, your dad is a criminal."

I lifted my gaze to his and gave a single nod.

"And you're working with him?"

"No!" I snapped from a burst of anger at being thrown in with him again. "Of course, I'm not–" I broke off because it wasn't true. It might have been true yesterday, but it wasn't anymore. I *was* working with my dad.

I blew out my breath. "He got himself into trouble with those guys you saw last night. They're holding him hostage until I do this job."

Hayes' expression cleared, like that explained everything to his satisfaction. "Okay." He nodded. "Okay, baby doll. I understand."

I blinked in confusion. "What do you understand?"

He rubbed his thumb across his lower lip. "I understand you were raised by a criminal. You went into law enforcement as a reaction to your upbringing, trying to stay on the side that was right, but now you have to risk everything, or someone dies."

Tears filled my eyes at his succinct summary.

"How'd I do?"

I let out a laughing sob, then covered my lips with my fingers. "Yeah. That about sums it up."

Hayes nodded. "I'm in."

I nearly choked on my own spit. My spine shot out straight, and I leaned forward. "What? *No,* Hayes. Absolutely not."

"Listen, baby doll. You've been pushing me away from the start. I thought maybe it was because you had commitment issues. Maybe you'd been hurt before, and you were scared of it happening again. That was legit and all, and I hoped to wear you down. To let you see I wasn't like any guys in your past. But now I see you have genuine, serious problems. The kind I can help you with. So, I sure as hell am going to help get you out of your pickle."

"Pickle?" I asked, huffing out a laugh.

"How about cluster fuck? When we're done figuring your shit out, you can stop hiding who you are from me. Because I already know. And I've already accepted it."

Jesus.

I shook my head, pushed open the door and bolted. I ran past my car and down the road toward town. It was miles away and unless I was a marathon runner, I'd never get there. Except I had to run. Had to get away. The hat and wig flew off my head.

Hayes caught up to me, his long legs eating up the distance. He was fit–damn those SEALs–and wasn't even breathing hard. His arm snagged about my middle, and he lifted me right off my feet.

"Let me go!" I shouted, thrashing as if I was a fish caught on a hook. "Hayes, you have to let me go."

"No." He murmured in my ear. "You've gone on alone too long. It's time to stop running."

Tears threatened as sweat coated my skin. The sun beat down on us. God, I wanted to bawl like a baby. I'd never in my life had anyone just accept me for who I was, blemishes and all. My mom abandoned me when I needed her most. So had my dad. I hadn't let anyone get close enough to do it again.

But here was Hayes. Reaching across the ocean divide I tried to keep between us and wouldn't go away. This guy followed me thinking I was a criminal, then when he heard my story, offered to join me. Just like that. His honor be damned.

A tear slid down my cheek because I cared too much for him. The more I pushed him away, the more he'd stuck. I cared for him, dammit! "I can't let you do this, Hayes," I said, trying so damn hard to be brave. To be honorable when what I had to do was anything but.

He shrugged, and I felt it against my back. "Try to stop me."

I glanced over my shoulder at him, the reality of it dawning on me. I wouldn't be able to stop him. This guy was steadfast in his pursuit of me, and he'd be steadfast in his decision to help.

But there was no way in hell I'd let him risk his life, honor, reputation and team for the steaming pile of poop that was my situation right now. He might know about the job, but I had to wonder if he knew about my past. It had been sealed, and it'd been a secret for over a decade.

I couldn't let him get involved, but he wasn't letting me go. I couldn't save myself from what I had to do, but I could protect him from himself. No way was he stooping low with me.

So that meant there was only one thing to do—trick him.

Play along, let him think I was going to let him help, and leave him behind when the time came.

Good thing my dad had taught me how to lie at

the same time he taught me how to pick every lock, how to grift and how to steal.

I gave in. Wilted in his hold. I turned, and he loosened his grip, so I remained in his arms. Tilting my head back, I looked up at him. "Thank you," I whispered.

He instantly cupped my nape and pulled me forward to drop a kiss on the top of my head. "You're not alone, Megan. We'll handle this. Together."

I closed my eyes and nodded.

Like hell we would.

CHAPTER
SEVENTEEN

HAYES

I DIDN'T LIKE IT.

I scrubbed a hand across my face and stared down at the house plans again. I'd shown up at Megan's the next night when she got off work to go over her plans for the job. We'd had pizza delivered and opened a couple of beers, and we sat at her kitchen table now, nursing the drinks and going over the details.

I'd had Kennedy and the guys researching the hell out of this guy Burns today, trying to find out where he might be holding Megan's dad. If Alpha Mountain

Security could extract Colin Hager before Megan ever got her hands dirty, it would solve everything. So far, we'd come up short, but I was still holding out hope. We extracted oil tycoons and diplomats from the shittiest hell holes on the planet. We could find a deadbeat dad being held prisoner somewhere in the northwest.

"So, you cut the security and drop in through the skylight into a room with laser detectors. Then you're supposed to hang upside down from the rooftop while you disable the security on the glass case, pick the lock, grab the Viking blade and escape the way you came?"

Megan nodded. "Yeah."

Christ. I hated the whole plan. Especially the part about her going in solo. SEALs didn't *do* solo.

"I don't like you going in alone while they're in the house. I did some research, Megan. Did you know this guy, Lucas Straight, is a major donor to the NRA? That means there are weapons in that mansion. Weapons he probably won't think twice to use if he catches you there. Especially not with Montana's Castle Law and Stand Your Ground and all that."

Megan's jaw flexed. "Everyone in Montana has a gun. What else is new?"

I gave her a look, and she added, "I won't get caught. I'm actually really good at this."

God, her voice sounded so heavy. It killed me. I'd do anything to lift the burden from her shoulders right now and carry it all.

"Why's that exactly?"

"My dad taught me everything, and I had *on-the-job* training." She made air quotes as she spoke. "Stealing from people was his job, how he made money."

"And he used you, a kid, to help." I wasn't sure if she even recognized how ridiculous what she was saying was. A man using a kid as a partner in crime.

She shrugged. "I didn't know any better. He made it fun. Until it wasn't."

She looked at the plans, but it was obvious she wasn't seeing them.

"What happened?" I reached out, took her hand in mine. Her dark gaze lifted. She licked her lips.

"A job a lot like this one. Ironic, isn't it?" The corner of her mouth turned up. "The Empress ring. Go ahead, look it up."

I didn't take my eyes off hers. "I'd rather you tell me than the Internet."

"I had to climb through ducts to get to it. I rappelled down and picked the lock on the case. Got it even. Somehow, the system came back online. I was caught."

Jesus.

"Did a year in juvie."

I leaned back in my chair and wiped a hand down my face. "Where you got your GED." It all made sense now. "Your record is sealed."

She nodded. "I was a minor. When I got out at eighteen, I steered as far away from my father as I could."

"Police academy."

"Yeah."

"Let me guess what happened with your dad. Nothing."

She popped to her feet and paced her small kitchen. I wasn't even sure if she knew her action was so telling. That she was still riled, still pissed after all this time. Hell, who wouldn't be?

"He bolted. I was caught. Since I was a minor, I got a slap on the wrist."

"A year in juvenile detention is a *slap on the wrist*?" I asked. "It must have been hell."

She stilled and frowned.

I leaned forward and set my forearms on the table. "Baby doll, you're going to risk everything for a man–your father–who abandoned you? Who left you to take the fall for his actions? A kid?"

Tear-filled eyes looked at me. Stuck. Caught in a vicious cycle. I understood family, the need to help them, but I'd decided to steer clear of the ones who'd gone bad. Her dad was all she had, but he'd fucking *abandoned* her in a way far worse than her mom.

"I can't let him die," she admitted.

"Your mom left. I get that. But your dad *used* you. He's using you now."

Her gaze narrowed, and she glared. "You don't think I know that?"

She was caught, and there was nothing I could do but help her. If Burns killed her father, she'd have to live with that for the rest of her life. Sure, it wouldn't have been her fault, but she wouldn't see it that way.

"Fine. Let's talk about a different way in though." I turned the blueprints around, studying the tiny print outlining the security at each entrance.

She shook her head and dropped back into her chair. "There isn't one. I've researched it. My dad researched it. If there were another way, my dad would've done the job on his own. That skylight is the only possible entrance to his treasure room."

"What do you know about Burns and his operations?" I asked. "Do you think he's in Spokane right now or somewhere in Montana waiting for you to finish this job? Any ideas on where he'd keep your dad?"

Megan joined her hands together and leaned her jaw on her knuckles, considering. After a long moment of silence, she shook her head. "I really don't know. I haven't seen these guys since I was a teenager, and even then, it was very limited. It's not like my dad and Burns are friends. He is a dangerous business partner—that's all."

"If you had to guess," I pressed. "Montana or Washington? Where is he right now?"

She scrubbed both hands up her cheeks and dragged them down again. "Montana, probably. They'd stay close to watch me. Make sure I'm doing what I'm supposed to."

"I have Kennedy trying to hack his credit card records to see if we can find anything that way," I told her. Left out that that wasn't the only thing he was hacking. We didn't leave a detail uncovered. If we did, it was how we ended up dead.

Her brows shot up. "Wow. Can he do that?"

"Unlike you in law enforcement, we don't have to stick within the confines of the law. With time, he'll get answers. But the sooner we can close in on

Burns, the better. I'd like to extract your dad before you–we–go in."

She went still, watching me, then swallowed. "You can't just extract my dad. He owes Burns a lot of money. He won't stop coming for him–or me."

This was the hitch in my plan. Megan was right. I didn't know her dad's skill set, but Megan was an asset for the guy. If she could steal a fucking dagger like she planned, she could do other jobs too. I saw blackmail in her future.

Burns might need to be... permanently eliminated... because no one threatened my woman. It was something I'd been turning over in my mind.

I was a sniper for the SEALs. I'd been given directives to eliminate dangerous targets before. Would this be much different?

On one hand, every one of my kills had been ordered by my government. This one? Definitely off the books, which meant, it wouldn't be legal.

On the other hand, this guy was a killer. He'd threatened to kill Megan. Was I going to let him live when my woman's life was at risk?

Fuck no. So yeah, I was willing to let my honor get tarnished a little in the name of saving Megan from a murderous prick.

I nodded. "Yeah, I get that." I cleared my throat. "I'm going to take care of him."

"How?" Megan demanded, arching a brow.

"Since you're an officer of the law, I don't think I'll be sharing those plans with you."

Megan's eyes rounded and took on a haunted quality. She pressed her fingertips to her mouth. "Hayes." Her voice sounded scratchy and hoarse. "I can't let you do that."

"Why the hell not?"

Megan's shoulders sagged, and she looked over her beer at me with pure despair. "I don't want you to break the law for me, Hayes. I can't ask that of you."

"You're not asking," I said fiercely. "I work for a security firm. This is the kind of shit we handle. Doing things when law enforcement can't. Hell, who do you think hires us? So, if we can handle it, we're going to."

She set her beer on the table. "Right. Well, I was raised by a cat burglar." She tapped the plans for the mansion. "This is the kind of shit I can handle."

We had a stare-off across the table.

"Give me a few more days to try to find your dad," I said. "If we can't find him, then we go forward with your plan."

Megan nodded and pushed back from the table. "You staying?" she asked over her shoulder as she walked out of the kitchen.

Part of me wanted to rage at her. *Hell, yes, I was staying. Every. Fucking. Night.*

Had she not figured that out yet? Had she not figured out I was in this for the long haul? That she'd never be alone again?

I knew she was stressed and tired and had a habit of pushing people away, but asking if I was staying wasn't letting me in. She wanted sex. To lose herself in the pleasure I gave her.

That was the kicker. *I gave her* the escape she needed. I was the escape. She just didn't see it that way yet. I let it go–for now–and followed her into the bedroom.

I leaned against the doorway with my arms folded across my chest as she stripped out of her clothes.

She came to me, naked. Beautiful. "I'm sorry." Her hands went to my belt buckle and worked it open.

I watched her, not touching yet. "What for?"

"I didn't want you involved."

Dammit.

I snagged her around the waist and yanked her

ALPHA MOUNTAIN: REBEL 171

up against my body. "I'm *involved*," I growled. "You're involved, that means I'm involved. No fucking way I'd leave you high and dry on this, baby doll."

She said nothing, just dropped to her knees and took my cock out.

Fuck me. I wrapped her hair around my fist as she tucked the head in her mouth and sucked. Her lips looked so incredible stretched around my thick member, taking me deeper and all the way to the back of her throat. She used her hand, fisting the base and dragging it in concert with the movement of her mouth, so it felt like she had all of me in deep.

I let out a groan. Sweet Jesus it felt so good. I wanted it to go on forever, but I was also already sweating, my balls heavy, my need thick.

Just when my thighs started quaking, she popped off and sat back on her heels. "Are you going to let me be in charge again tonight?"

No man in my position would've told her no. If she'd asked me to set my clothes on fire and dance on the roof, I would've said yes.

"That's right, baby doll. I'm *letting* you. I could toss you onto that bed and fuck you six ways to Sunday. But I can see you need to be in charge. I'll give you whatever you need."

Her eyes widened as she processed my words, at

what she'd said. I was dressed except for my hard dick out, while she was naked. Bare.

She nodded, then I let her lead me to the bed. I laid down and let her guide my arms above my head. When she handcuffed my wrists to the bed frame, I was already out of my mind with lust.

A spurt of pre-cum seeped from my slit, loving that she'd pulled out those fucking cuffs.

When she crawled over me and took me back in that sweet mouth of hers, I thought I'd died and gone to heaven. My hips bucked up even as I tried not to lunge down her throat.

"Hell, yes, baby doll. Just like that," I groaned. "Climb up on me and let me finish in that tight pussy."

"Nope," she said, looking up my body. "I'm in charge, remember? This one's for you."

She took me deep into the back of her throat, making enthusiastic sounds as I shook and grunted beneath her. Holy fuck, did she even have a gag reflex?

"I'm going to come, doll," I warned, but she still didn't come off, not until she'd brought me to a shouted orgasm and swallowed down every drop of my cum. I lay there, catching my breath, my eyes closed, soaked in pleasure, and she slipped off the bed.

I thought she'd gone to the bathroom.

It took me a solid sixty seconds before I realized Megan hadn't just left the bedroom.

"Megan?" I called.

She'd left the fucking house.

She'd handcuffed me to her bed and left.

And dammit–*I knew exactly where she was headed.*

CHAPTER EIGHTEEN

MEGAN

I HAD TO FOCUS, but it was nearly impossible. I'd left Hayes handcuffed to my bed. I'd used the one thing that was a constant between us as a weapon. The one place where I'd let go completely, giving myself to someone in the most intimate of ways. I'd pushed him away. Over and over.

He'd proven he would stick. That he'd play by my rules.

Yet I'd just changed them.

To protect him. The idiot.

He didn't belong on this job with me. If I got caught... well, I had before.

I was older now. Smarter. More skilled.

I was saving my father, but I wasn't relying on him for support.

No. I was relying on myself, the only person I could trust.

Except... I could trust Hayes.

I cut across the open field and stumbled over a rock.

"Dammit," I whispered. My mind wasn't on the task.

The dark house loomed in the distance, the light of the half-moon guiding me. It was a cool night, typical for summer this far north, but I was sweating. I'd grabbed clothes from my laundry room. Black ones I'd had on top of the dryer for the job. I hadn't thought I'd have to put them on in the garage or even handcuff Hayes to go solo.

I'd had no choice. The guy was like a golden retriever, willing to follow me blindly.

I shook my head as I hoofed it across the field. No, that wasn't remotely accurate. He was a Rottweiler. Quiet, loyal, yet fierce. Probably ruthless when faced with the enemy, but I had yet to see him that way.

He was going to be pissed. But it was better than

him behind bars. He wanted to protect me, but who the hell was going to take care of him?

I made it to the mansion and peeked in a window. A light over the stove in the kitchen was on. The house was completely dark. Not even a motion sensor spotlight on the exterior. It was used to deter robbers, but maybe this far out, they felt it wasn't necessary.

Except the rest of the place was wired like Fort Knox.

I adjusted the coiled length of rope over my shoulder and snuck to the side of the house. To the huge river rock chimney. The layout showed a huge fireplace in the great room, and this was my access. There would be no belaying, only free climbing.

I look up into the darkness, the stars twinkling, taking a moment. This was what I'd vowed never to return to. I was letting down the girl in juvie, who'd spent a miserable year a prisoner of her own actions and of the one man she'd thought would protect and care for her.

Except he hadn't.

Yet here I was, ready to do it all over again, to risk everything. For the same man.

It seemed so stupid when I had a good man, a trustworthy, honorable one, handcuffed to my bed. A man who wanted to be there for me. It had been the only way to stop him.

He was what I needed in my life. Someone steadfast, who cared about me. Who was willing to give up all of his hard-fought values. For me.

I blinked back tears. No. *Suck it up, Megan. He's not yours. He'll never be yours. Especially not now. When he gets himself free, he'll be done with me. He knew the truth now. I was trouble. I lacked honor. I was everything he hated.*

Hayes would hate me eventually if he didn't already hate me now. I sniffed, reached for the smooth, round rocks above my head, and set my foot on a low one. I'd come full circle. This was me. Right here.

A thief. Alone.

CHAPTER
NINETEEN

HAYES

"THE HELICOPTER WOULD HAVE COME in handy," I grumbled, my hand on the *oh shit* bar above my head.

Ford glanced my way for a split second then back on the road, taking it almost twice the speed limit. He'd returned from D.C. with no additional intel, and that had made him cranky. And his driving a little wild.

"It would if there weren't a chance of snagging power lines or fencing or hell... running into a fucking mountain."

I'd never been so antsy before a mission before.

We had guns, but we weren't pulling them from the SUV. There was no enemy here. The Straights weren't the bad guys. Megan was.

So was I because I was going to help her break into their house. My team had insisted on backing me up, even though I'd told them this wasn't their fight.

It was a stupid fucking Viking dagger. He had insurance. Hell, I'd even steal it back from Burns and give it back to the actor personally. This wasn't a mission where a kidnapped kid needed to be rescued from militants who planned to behead him as an example of power.

We were in Montana—not Mosul.

The SUV bumped down the dirt road.

"As she already deduced, the only reasonable access for her is the skylight," Kennedy said from the backseat. His laptop gave his face a blue glow, and his fingers flew over the keys. "VistaStar installed the security system after the Straights bought the property. Upgraded when he relocated the bulk of his Viking collection to the house. Retinal scanners. Biometrics. Other shit."

Just as Megan's dad had outlined.

Taft leaned forward between the front seats. "Tell me again how she got past you."

From the corner of my eye, I saw Ford's grin.

I ground my back molars and stayed silent. I'd had to break her headboard to get free of the cuffs. It still wasted precious time, and by the time I'd gotten to my truck and gunned it back to the ranch, Megan had a significant head start.

I should've followed her directly, but I needed equipment. My team came without me asking. They'd just suited up with me, as if it was assumed they were going.

"In all the times we trained to get out of restraints, I don't remember once having my dick out," Taft added with a laugh.

"When's the last time you got your dick sucked, asshole?" I growled. "I'm guessing never. I have to wonder if you still have your V card."

Kennedy snickered.

"Says the man who's in love with a thief," Taft countered. "She better be fucking worth it."

I spun around as best I could in my seat belt and glared.

"You're going to find your woman, and then you're going to eat every fucking word because you'll do whatever it takes to protect her."

Taft held up his hands in surrender. "Helping her steal a knife is child's play. This is gonna be fun."

I didn't think *fun* was the word, but this wouldn't be the hardest mission we'd completed. Which was ironic since I was ready to rip Taft's head off before I officially broke the law.

"Here's the info on that other robbery," Kennedy said. "An attempted theft on the Empress Ring happened eleven years ago. It says the burglar entered through the HVAC system, rappelled down over the locked case and stole it, but was captured exiting the boiler room. The ring was safely returned and, from what I can tell, is now a part of a collection at a museum in Venice."

What she told me earlier had been true.

"Your woman's quite the cat burglar," Kennedy added.

"No mention of accomplices?" I asked.

"No."

"She did a stint in juvie while Daddy got away, and now she's doing an almost identical job to save him?" Taft asked.

"Burns is going to kill him if she doesn't," I explained. "It doesn't matter the reason. My woman's going in alone, and that's not fucking okay."

Ford slows the SUV. "Easy, brother. We have your back. And hers."

"I'm going to spank her ass for going this alone."

"We don't fall for meek women," Ford added. "We'd be bored out of our minds."

"Yeah, infiltration and extraction on a Thursday night?" Taft asked. "Hooyah."

"We're close," Ford said, a few minutes later.

I grab my comms unit from the center console and stuff it in my ear. "Testing, testing."

"Clear," Kennedy responds as Ford pulls over and cuts the engine.

"The house is over there." I point out the windshield into the darkness and unclick my seat belt. It helped that I'd followed Megan here earlier. The guys only had the info Kennedy found online and the plans I'd shared–the ones I'd nabbed from Megan's kitchen table after I'd gotten myself free of the cuffs.

"We know the plan. Go get your woman," Ford said.

I nodded then slipped out into the darkness.

I wasn't kidding when I told the guys Megan was going to get a spanking. I'd let her run the show enough. Held secrets. Kept herself apart. Her heart too. That shit was ending now. If she hadn't figured out I was sticking, she'd learn tonight. It was time she knew who was in charge, and it sure as fuck wasn't her.

CHAPTER
TWENTY

MEGAN

ONCE I GOT to the roof by scaling the Straights' chimney, I looped the rope I'd tied off at the ground over the roof vent for one of the toilets. I let the rest of it drop the two stories to the ground ready to be used later. From there, I scaled the roof until I came to the skylight. I thought about the blueprint and realized this was the one over the central stairwell, not the room with the dagger.

The shingles were rough beneath my palms, and I moved slowly so as not to slip. With the treads on my shoes, I held well, but the incline was more generous than other roofs I'd had to maneuver in the past.

I was also older. I hadn't grown since I was seventeen although my hips and boobs definitely had. But it was clear I wasn't as agile. No, that wasn't right. I stopped at the correct skylight and took a breath. Back in the day, I'd been fearless. Had a sense of indestructibility I didn't have now. Maybe it was the fact that I'd been caught, that I wasn't invincible, that had me moving more cautiously now.

I had to be methodical. Consistent. To let my skills take over. I was ballsy and confident enough to be on someone's roof at midnight. I could do the rest.

Using a penknife, I cut the seal around the edges of the skylight, then worked a slim chisel in to pry it open.

Once open, I tugged off the second rope. This one was thinner. I tied it off like my escape rope and attached the clip to my harness I'd had on over my dark clothes. Checking to make sure I had the tools I needed in my pockets, I leaned into the opening and tumbled through. My harness caught me as I dangled in the vaulted ceiling.

The Straights, at least Mrs. Straight who I'd met earlier, was here. Fortunately, the master bedroom was on the ground floor and at the other side of the house. With my pen light, I swept the beam around the room below me. If I were a fan of Viking history, I'd have probably creamed myself. Helmets, artwork and other old trinkets were beneath cases and on the white walls. I couldn't appreciate any of it, especially since my father's life was at stake.

All of the Vikings were dead and wouldn't miss a dagger. The Straights were well insured and would be compensated for the theft. It was my father's life's value that laid beneath me, the jewels glinting in the gold hilt.

Slowly, I dropped into the room until my feet touched the wood floor. I didn't release the rope as I stepped up to the display. Sticking the pen light in my mouth so it aimed onto the glass, I pulled out my tools and got to work. The lock was similar to the one for the Empress ring, only the security features were newer. I pulled out the slim piece of metal and slid it into the wedge I'd made. I took a breath as I raised the glass, hoping the metal would do its job by continuing the electrical circuit.

Alarms didn't go off, so I exhaled. Feeling like Indiana Jones and the golden statue, my fingers itched to pluck the dagger from the velvet, but I studied it for a moment to ensure there wasn't a secondary sensor. I lifted it, felt the heft of the ancient weapon, then tucked the hilt into the belt at my waist.

On the side of the case, a red light came on.

"Shit," I whispered, my heart rate kicking into gear. With a calmness I was trying hard to maintain, I set the glass back in place, hoping there was only a timer with the lid remaining off.

With the cover down, I couldn't see the light, but it was an indication I'd been here long enough.

Pulling the climbing ascenders up the rope where I'd been affixed them earlier, I gripped one, then the other and started to pull myself up the twenty feet to the open skylight.

I didn't have tons of upper body strength. The bulk of my consistent workout to stay in shape involved running and target shooting. I could rock climb, but my skill set wasn't much on rocks–although it had come in handy for the chimney–but ropes themselves.

One over the other, I worked my way up the rope. All was fine until I thought I'd clipped one in and hadn't. My weight shifted, and I dropped, wrenching my left shoulder. I dangled far over the floor as I winced in pain.

Spinning, I whipped my arm around to snag the

rope to try again. I got it into place, ready to pull myself up, but my strength was seriously flagging.

You can do it. One hand over the other. You're almost there.

My gloved fingers slipped on the rope, and I dropped another six inches.

Fuck!

I drew a breath in across my teeth and let go of my right hand to reach as far up as I could. I only had a few more pulls in me. I needed to get to the top before my strength gave out.

I nearly screamed when a strong hand clasped mine and pulled hard, lifting me up through the opening.

I'd been caught! Fuckity fuck fuck!

But no.

It was Hayes's warm brown eyes I met as I scrabbled onto the roof. The instantaneous relief–joy even–was short-lived. Because then I panicked in a completely different way. Hayes was here. On the roof! Risking everything for me.

He didn't release my hand as his gaze swept over me, as if checking to make sure I'd made it out in one piece. I'd never seen him look this way before. His gaze was intense. His jaw clenched. Every part of his body—that I could see—was rigid with tension and focus.

The air was cool and felt good on my heated skin. I recognized Hayes's scent on the breeze.

"Get the glass back in place." His voice was barely a whisper as he pulled the rope up through the opening. For someone so large, he moved along the roof with impressive agility. As I settled the skylight closed and removed the metal grounding piece, I watched him coil the rope and move to the chimney. With his feet, he braced himself between the angled roof and the rising stones.

"Did you get it?" he whispered.

I nodded, pointing to my hip. He looked there then moved.

Hand over hand, he lowered himself down the side of the chimney with the rope I'd had ready. It had been for my departure, but he'd clearly used it to scale the house. He went first, probably figuring I couldn't escape him if he stood at the bottom of the rope. He wasn't wrong.

I rappelled after him and felt his hands at my waist to lower me the last few feet. Reaching down, I untied the rope from the hose spigot, then pulled and pulled until the section we'd just used to lower ourselves went up to the roof and around the vent to fall to my feet.

Collecting the entire rope, I tucked it under my arm as best I could, but Hayes snagged it from me. He took my wrist and pulled me away from the house. He wasn't running, but his legs were much longer than mine. I had to move all out to keep up.

"Package received," he murmured, his gaze scanning the darkness. I assumed *I* was the package, and he had some fancy communications device on him. I guessed SEALs were never alone. "Extraction in five minutes."

I didn't know who he was talking to, but it seemed I wasn't the only one used to late-night missions. He skirted the back of the property, around the large patio and landscaped backyard to the field beyond.

A coyote howled in the distance, but other than that, it was silent. I didn't know how a man of his size could move so silently, but he was a SEAL.

We moved for a few minutes. From my visit earlier, I knew we were doing a wide arc around the property and aiming for the road. We hit the packed dirt and an engine started nearby. An SUV stopped before us, lights off. Hayes opened the rear door and all but pushed me in. He tossed the rope into my lap then climbed in beside me.

On my other side was Kennedy. Ford and Taft were in the front.

The SUV sped off.

"Hey there, Deputy," Taft said. "You've got some fancy moves."

"If you're looking for a job outside of law enforcement..." Ford told me but left it hanging.

Kennedy winked. "Welcome to the team."

CHAPTER
TWENTY-ONE

HAYES

"ARE YOU PISSED?" Megan asked as I parked her Subaru in her driveway. Her voice is quiet and unsure, which is not something I like. I like her ballsy and prickly, and I admit, stealthily stealing a stupid historic knife and getting out undetected.

She could be a SEAL or in the circus.

We'd picked up her car after we extracted her from the heist location, and I had insisted on driving. I was all for my woman taking care of herself, but I drove. End of story.

I hadn't said anything on the ride back to town. I was the kind of guy who went silent when a lot was going on in my head, and I didn't know where to start.

"Not pissed." I climbed out of the car and strode to her door, which I'd left unlocked when I dashed out earlier. Sure, shit could have gotten stolen, but the only thing I worried about inside her house was Megan herself. Since she hadn't been there and instead had been breaking into a fucking house...

She followed me in. "Because you seem kind of pissed."

She carefully removed the five-million-dollar dagger from her hip pocket and put it in her gun safe.

I kept walking until I got to the bedroom–the place where she'd tried to keep me from following her just a few hours ago. It felt like a lifetime, already.

I toed off my boots then stripped out of my shirt.

Megan surveyed the broken headboard. "Guess it takes more than a pair of puny handcuffs to stop a SEAL."

I grunted in response.

"I'm going to take a shower," she said when I didn't respond further.

"Yeah." I followed her into the bathroom. Washing off the night's deed suited me, too.

We didn't say a word as we stood under the shower spray together. Her tub was fucking tiny. I let her soap me then took the bar from her and returned the favor. She watched me all the while, her brows knit tight.

It was the most attentive she'd been to me. Usually, I was the one focused on her, and she was deflecting. I was up in my head, trying to figure out what I had to do or say or be to finally get through to her. To show her I was going to stick. She couldn't stop me from coming for her, no matter what she tried to do to me.

Handcuffs to me were nothing more than part of a magician's act.

If what happened wasn't enough to drive that concept home for her, I had no fucking clue what would.

I turned off the water and stepped out, grabbing a towel for Megan. Her eyes went soft at the gesture, like me handing it to her meant something. Like I wouldn't always take care of her needs first, until the day I died.

She was fucking surprised I was here. That I was being nice. That I was her man. And that confusion was my fucking issue.

I used my own towel and returned to the bedroom.

"Hayes, I'm sorry." She spoke behind me. "I didn't want to entangle you in my mess. You're an honorable man. If something had gone wrong tonight, and you had been caught–"

"That was for me to decide." I whirled and reached for her.

She stood with the towel tucked around her ripe breasts, her hair still dripping. She stepped into me, bringing her hands to my bare chest, but I captured her wrists. I used them to spin her around and pin them behind her back, folding her torso over the bed. It was reminiscent–but a much gentler version–of the badass move I'd seen her perform on the traffic stop with that drunk on the side of the road.

For once, she didn't fight as I held her in place. There was no wrestling match this time. No competition between us that I let her win. I was having my way tonight, and we both knew it. I held her two wrists in one hand and used the other to pull off her towel.

I clapped a heavy hand down on her ass, making her startle and squirm. I repeated the action on the other cheek then stopped to rub away the red prints left by my fingers. "When are you going to get it through your beautiful head that I'm here for you?"

I spanked her again, hard enough to make her jerk.

"Hmm?"

Another spank.

"Hayes."

"Rafael."

I spanked her again.

"I'm here to stick, Megan. I'm not going anywhere."

I slapped her again.

"I'm not going to abandon you like your mom and dad did. If you have problems, I'm going to share them. Help you with them. You don't think I'm strong enough to handle them?"

She didn't answer, only whimpered. If she'd told me to stop, to let her up, I'd have released her instantly. But it seemed she needed to have me do this, to hear what I had to say. To take the punishment she deserved.

That she needed because no one else had stuck around to give one to her.

I delivered three more hard spanks.

"Now climb up on that bed, I'm going to fuck you until know you're mine."

I knew it was true when Megan scampered to obey. She may be a world-class cat burglar and a badass sheriff's deputy. She may have refused me a first or second date, pushed me away at every turn, and handcuffed me to her fucking bed to keep me from following—to *protect* me—but right now, at this moment, she was my woman. Eager to make things right. Ready to receive me.

I grabbed a condom from my wallet, ripped it open, and rolled it on before climbing over her. Vulnerability flickered in Megan's eyes as she glanced at me.

I gave her a hard kiss. A claiming kiss.

I'd been patient. I'd taken things at her pace. But I was done. She was mine, and I was going to fuck her so hard she'd remember it for days.

My tongue swept between her lips at the same time the head of my cock nudged at her entrance. She reached down to grasp my dick and tucked the head inside her entrance.

"Fuck," I groaned at how wet she was. From nothing but a hard spanking.

Then I couldn't hold back. I speared her with a hard thrust, sinking all the way in to the hilt, then drawing back and thrusting again. Her head flew toward the broken headboard, and I caught her by the nape to keep her from hitting it.

"That's right, baby doll. You're going to take every inch of me tonight, aren't you?" I growled.

"Yes," she breathed. "Yes, Rafael."

Fuck, yes! She finally said my name, and damn if it didn't make my dick even harder to hear it from her gorgeous lips. Her head was tossed back, her eyes closed. Her wet hair was a tangle on the pillow.

I drilled into her, already at a finishing speed, even though we'd just started. The need to fully own her flushed me with heat.

"Who's going to satisfy you?" I demanded.

"You are," she gasped.

I fucked her harder.

"Who's going to make you come?"

Her eyes fly open. "You are."

"That's right, baby doll. Every. Fucking. Night. And who's going to stick through thick and thin?"

The cry that escaped her lips sounded pained, but I knew it wasn't from the physical pounding I was giving her. It was the emotional one. I was demanding something from her. Serving it up. Making her see what was real and true between us. What we needed. What we were. What we could be.

"Say it," I gritted, sweat beading on my forehead. My balls were heavy stones, ready to release.

"You are, Rafael." She arched up, her cunt squeezing tight around my dick as she came.

"Oh no, baby doll. I'm not nearly done with you," I said, when she was done. I pulled out and rolled her over to her belly. I entered her from behind, loving the new angle, the way my cock bottomed out along her front wall, making her moan-cry with pleasure. Just looking down at her, seeing the long line of her spine, her upturned ass all red from her spanking, the way her lips were spread around my thrusting dick...

"You're gonna take it from me all night long, baby doll. I'm going to make you remember who you belong with."

"Yes...yes." Her hoarse, throaty cries nearly drove me wild. I arced in and out of her, riding my own wave of pleasure until the pressure grew too great. "You gonna come for me again, baby doll? Squeeze my dick up tight and make me shout?" I reached around the front of her hips. Sliding my hand under to rub her clit.

She screamed, convulsing beneath me with a violent climax. I shoved in tight, my loins pressing against her heated ass cheeks and savored the sensation of her tight, pulsing squeezes. As soon as she was done, I let go, held myself deep and filled the condom. Pulse after pulse of cum came from my balls. One of these days we'd forgo condoms so nothing was between us, and I'd mark her as mine. Inside and out.

I pulled out, rid myself of the condom in the bathroom then returned. She scrambled onto her knees and faced me. I walked to her, and she wrapped her arms around me like vines and burst into tears.

Keeping her close, I settled on the bed with her on top of me and let her cry. I didn't know how long she'd held them in. Maybe since her dad had left her to fend for herself when she'd been caught stealing the ring. Maybe when her mom skipped out on her. I had no idea and it didn't matter.

I was here, and she could cry all she wanted.

CHAPTER
TWENTY-TWO

MEGAN

HAYES LEFT at eight the next morning. It was the first night I didn't kick him out of my bed and out of my house.

He stayed, and for the first time ever, I slept in a man's arms. I breathed in his scent and was enveloped in his strength.

It had been hard to look him in the eye this morning because not only had I cried all over him, but he'd also spanked my ass.

And I'd liked it.

I was game for all kinds of things when it came to sex, but that spanking he'd delivered had been different. He'd been punishing me, not for breaking into a house and stealing something but because I'd done it alone. I'd kept it a secret and kept him out of it, out of my life.

I felt raw and exposed and confused. But also... whole.

As I poured my second cup of coffee and stared out my back window, I couldn't remember feeling less alone. He wasn't even here, and I felt like Hayes was mine.

No, Raf.

He was everything I never expected. Never knew could be mine.

He was–

A pounding on the front door had me spilling my coffee.

"Shit," I muttered.

I'd planned to call Burns this morning to meet him, but it seemed he beat me to it. The last thing I wanted to do was face him, but I didn't need him catching my neighbors' attention.

I yanked the door open.

Just as I thought, it was the asshole along with his two goons.

And my father. *He* was a surprise.

"Dad!" I said. I wasn't a hugger and neither was

he, but I felt the need to reach out. I took his hand in mine and gave it a squeeze.

His face was all beat up. A cut was scabbed on his forehead. He had a black eye, and his lip was split. And the guy who'd meted it out was here with us. I wanted to punch *him* and see how he liked it.

"Hey, Meggie."

I glared at Burns who remained silent, entering into my living room just as he had the last time, like he owned the place. Or me.

"Heard on the police scanners about the robbery," Dad said with a triumphant smile. "I'm proud of you. I knew you could do it."

"With the right incentive," Burns added, not to be left out.

"I'll get you the dagger, and you can get the hell out of here," I snapped. "You'll have what you want to leave my father alone."

Burns didn't say anything, only narrowed his gaze. He didn't like being told off, probably especially not by a woman, but he stayed quiet. Raising his hand, he waved it to indicate I should do what I just said.

Turning on my heel, I went into the kitchen, opened my gun safe and retrieved the dagger.

Returning to the living room, I slapped it in Burns' hand.

"There. I retrieved it for you. Now leave me and my dad alone and get the hell out," I practically growled.

My dad came over, set his hand on my shoulder and smiled. His eyes shone bright with... pride? Affection? It had been years since I'd seen my dad look at me this way. All because I'd rescued him.

"Ah Meggie, I knew you could do it. Burns didn't believe me, but I had faith in you." He chuckled. "I taught you everything you know."

I agreed to a certain point. I knew how to break and enter because of him, but I'd moved on, chosen a different life all on my own. Because he sure as hell hadn't been there with me in juvie. He also didn't know anything but the easy life on the wrong side of the law.

"You should go, too," I told him. I was glad he was okay, glad that Burns had the dagger, but I wanted him gone. "I did what I had to. You're safe from this asshole. Now slink away like you always do and let me get back to my life."

He slowly shook his head. "See, Burns. A firecracker. I told you she'd be perfect for joining us."

I frowned. That wasn't what I expected to say.

Maybe a thanks or something. "What the hell are you talking about?"

"You don't think I'd ever let myself get caught, would you, Meggie?"

I blinked, suddenly very confused.

"I'm too smart for that. You are too, now. You learned it from the Empress job, I imagine. The year you were held."

"Held? I was arrested, put in juvenile detention," I countered. "Do you have any idea what that was like? What I had to do to survive?"

He patted my head as if I were a dog or a cranky child in need of a nap.

"You haven't been caught since," he replied.

"Because I haven't done anything to be put behind bars. I'm a sheriff's deputy if you've forgotten."

"And also a thief," Burns added. He raised his phone. "Here's a picture of you with the dagger." He swiped his screen. "Here's you saying you're the one who retrieved it from the Straights."

My stomach plummeted, and my pulse kicked into high gear. I was used to being level headed under pressure. Under danger. Except this–

Fuck.

"What the hell do you want?" I asked, getting to

the point. He didn't take those images to take down to the station and have me arrested.

"Join us," my father said.

"Join you?" I waved my finger between them. "Dad, he was holding you hostage."

"I think that law and order stuff has made you forget where you came from. I wasn't really his hostage. I knew the only way you'd steal that dagger was if someone you cared about was threatened. And since I'm the only person you have—"

Oh. My. God. My stomach seized up as tight as a fist.

"You set me up," I whispered.

My father shook his head. "It was a test to show Burns your skills. You passed."

My eyes widened. "Passed what? A bad guy test? That I care about you?"

"That you're an asset I want on my team," Burns added.

I'd heard the same thing last night from Kennedy. Ford had offered me a job–even jokingly– and Kennedy had welcomed me to their team. Their team was honorable, though. They protected people. And defended liberty. Their team was for good.

Burns was pure evil.

As I stared at my dad, who now seemed to be

everything I never expected, I realized I was in trouble.

Huge trouble. I'd saved my father–who'd used me over and over–while I pushed Hayes away. My father stood before me and had not only gotten me to do a job for him, but he'd done it to show off my abilities to Burns.

What kind of fucked up mind did I have?

If I got caught, I'd go to jail. His hands, and Burns', would stay clean. If I succeeded, which I had, they got the dagger and a patsy. Me.

"I don't want to join you." I set my jaw, realizing it was probably too little, too late. "I want you out of my house. Out of my life. I'm done with you, Dad. I never want to see you again."

"Is it the cuts and bruises?" he asked, putting his fingers to the wounds on his face. "I thought it was a nice touch. It doesn't hurt if you're too drunk to remember being punched."

He'd gotten himself beat up as part of this plan? Holy fuck.

"You'll be joining us, Megan Hager," Burns said.

I shook my head. "No way."

"Or you can go to jail. A tip about who stole the dagger, and you'll be arrested. You think a movie star is going to let charges drop? Imagine the news in this quaint little town. *Deputy is really a jewel thief.* You'll do time. In a real prison, not day care for kids. I wonder how the general population will feel about a law enforcement officer in their mix?"

"I go work for you, or I go to jail," I stated, making sure I understood what he was saying.

"I told you she was smart," my father said. "Stop playing one of the good guys, Meggie. I raised you to be better than that."

"It's my job to uphold the law."

"And yet you broke it," he countered. "All by yourself. It took you long enough, but you showed your true colors."

I had. I'd made a choice to commit a crime.

For him.

For nothing.

"Pack your things," Burns ordered. "I'll text you the address in Spokane where you need to be tomorrow. I've got a job for you."

The goons, who'd been quiet all this time, opened the front door for Burns, and he strode out, taking the dagger with him. My dad set his hand on my shoulder and leaned in. "It'll be like old times, Meggie. We're going to have so much fun."

I heard the door close behind him as I stood there.

What had I done?

I ran for the bathroom and threw up the coffee that had curdled in my stomach. I messed up. So badly.

What was I going to do?

I couldn't arrest Burns. He hadn't done anything wrong. Sure, he had a stolen dagger, but he had proof I took it. Had he even had a buyer for it?

Probably. The one thing that man wanted was money.

I sat on the tile floor, leaned against the side of my tub, knee bent. I set my head on it.

My dad had organized this whole thing. He wanted me back in the business, and he'd used my emotions against me. I'd hated him for so long, I should have told him no. I had, but I'd let my feelings, my love for him, sway me.

I was a doormat. An idiot. I couldn't even love the right people.

Instantly, I thought of Hayes. Of loving him. Because while the sex the night before had been kinky and dirty as it had ever been between us, it had been intimate. I'd given myself to him. Opened up. Cried. Admitted I wanted to be with him.

Except that was never to be.

He'd spent the past week having sex with the

good Megan. The law enforcement officer. The one who'd broken into someone's house and robbed them because I cared about someone. I'd thought I was honorable, but I'd been wrong.

I'd ruined my life all on my own. I couldn't go back to work. I'd go to jail. No question.

If my father allowed himself to get beat up as part of a ruse to play at my emotions and get me to commit a crime, there was no question he'd turn me in if it kept him free.

Burns wasn't related and would do so in a heartbeat. He no doubt hated the police and seeing an officer take the fall for a crime? It'd make his day.

I had to go to work for him. At least until I could figure out how to bring them down. But then, would it be too late? Would I have committed enough crimes by then that I'd be complicit?

And Hayes?

God, Hayes.

I couldn't pull him into this. He'd proven last night he was willing to corrupt his honor for me. He'd been on that roof!

He was good. His entire team was. They'd dedicated years of their lives to the service of the country. Willingly served knowing they might die. Now, they did security. *Good* things.

I couldn't taint him.

I didn't deserve Hayes, and he sure as hell was too good for me.

No. I had to go. To leave.

Now.

I pushed to my feet and saw myself in the mirror over the vanity.

"You've been alone before. You'll be fine. You survived once. You can survive again."

Except I hadn't had Hayes before. He hadn't spanked my ass and told me he was there for me. He hadn't fucked me and told me I was his. He hadn't held me as I cried.

I had to do the one thing to Hayes that had destroyed me when I was seventeen.

I had to walk away from him. Abandon him.

Unlike what my father did for me, it was for his own good.

Because Megan Hager was all bad.

CHAPTER
TWENTY-THREE

HAYES

SHE WASN'T HOME. The alarm was set, but she wasn't inside.

The house was silent except for the hum of the fridge. She hadn't answered my text about having dinner at Alpha Mountain because Mrs. L was making that pot roast she promised. She hadn't answered the one I texted a few minutes ago.

Her car was gone. I went and opened her safe–watching her type in the numbers didn't require SEAL training–and her gun was gone. So was the Viking dagger.

"Fuck," I muttered.

It was supposed to be there until we met with Burns to get her father back.

Had she gone on her own?

"Son of a bitch."

Of course, she had. Why would she change the way she did things–alone–after what we shared the night before?

Hadn't I made myself fucking clear?

I pulled out my cell, dialed Kennedy.

"Yo."

"Pull up the feed on Megan's place. Work backward and see when she leaves."

"Hooyah."

I hear his fingers clacking on the keyboard. I paced her space, waiting to know what she'd done. A coffee cup was on the kitchen table. Her bed's not made.

"Her car pulls out of the garage at three twenty-two."

"She alone?"

"Affirmative."

More clacking.

"Hang on. Ten minutes earlier, she's out front on the phone."

"Can you play it for me?"

"Yeah, let me turn the speaker up."

Ten seconds later, I hear Megan's voice through my cell. It's a little rough since it's not live, but I could hear her clearly.

"Of course, I got it. Don't question my skills. No, there weren't any issues. I'll bring you the dagger only after I see my cut in my account." There's a pause. I wished I could see her face. "You don't believe I have it? I assume you called me because you heard of it over the police scanners. I might work for the Sparks sheriff's department, but the Straight place is out of my jurisdiction." Another pause. "I'm always up for another job. You think I can retire at forty on a deputy's salary? Right. I'll be there in two hours."

"That's it," Kennedy said. "She ends the call and goes back inside. Then she leaves."

Holy shit. I tugged on my hair and spun in a circle.

"Can you track her phone?"

More tapping. "Headed toward Missoula."

"Or, headed toward Spokane," I snarled. "And Burns."

I grabbed her coffee mug and tossed it at the wall. It shattered and pieces flew around the room.

"Get back here, and we'll figure this out," Kennedy said.

"Figure it out? What's there to figure out? She was in on it the whole time! Kept pushing me away because she didn't want me snooping. Jesus, I'm a fucking idiot."

"Get back here," he repeated. "We'll be waiting."

He hung up, and I grabbed hold of the edge of her counter and leaned against it. Tried not to lose my shit.

The one woman I let in, the one woman I wanted to be mine, and she turned out to be a fucking criminal. A user. Yeah, she'd fucking used me.

I'd stayed away from my family to keep from getting sucked into criminal activities, but here I'd gone and done exactly what I was trying to avoid in Sparks. For a woman.

A woman who didn't even profess to love me!

Up until the night before, she'd pushed me away. Tried to keep me at a distance, but last night?

"Fuck!" I shouted then stormed out of her house, the front door slamming behind me.

CHAPTER
TWENTY-FOUR

MEGAN

I DROVE WITHOUT STOPPING–HOURS on the highway. My body was made of lead. My mouth full of ash. It was incredible how different my entire life seemed from ten hours before. Just this morning–a lifetime ago–I'd woken up in Hayes' arms. We'd shared something intimate. Something big. Foolish me, I thought we were going to somehow handle Burns together and then ride into the sunset.

Now, I face a future of breaking the law. Living in the margins. Never knowing love.

No, that wasn't true. I'd known love.

I'd known it, and I just choked the life out of it.

I put a hand on my roiling stomach. I hadn't eaten all day, and I still couldn't. If I did, I'd just puke again.

That was what leaving Hayes made me feel like.

What hurting him did to me.

Because I knew when he pulled that feed from my porch, he was going to feel the worst kind of betrayal. A betrayal he didn't deserve.

I remembered Hayes had told me he'd tapped into my security system. That was how he'd learned about Burns, how he'd stunned me when he told me he knew all about the job. I hadn't given him any answers. He and the other guys with Alpha Mountain had put it all together. Like detectives. Like SEALs.

That meant I had to hide not only from Burns and my father but from Hayes as well. Even though it destroyed me–utterly and completely–I hoped my fake phone call had made him hate me. I needed to be sure he'd let it go.

So I'd had to do more than just a fake call. I had to go to Spokane, or at least in that direction, so their snooping would back up my words. I was Burns' partner in crime, and I was headed to join him in

Washington. Then Hayes would leave me alone. For good.

For *his* good.

I'd stolen a five-million-dollar dagger. Me. My father and Burns probably had alibis in different states for the time of the crime. If I contacted the authorities–even with me being a sheriff's deputy–I couldn't be sure anyone would believe me. Not with the evidence Burns held.

I'd made it all day without crying. Now I could let it out. Give into the tears clogging my throat.

Except they didn't flow. I was too numb. Too in shock. Too far removed from the Megan Hager I'd been yesterday to even cry.

My heart was too damaged. Too broken.

I had absolutely nothing.

And only now–now that I'd lost everything–could I see just how much Hayes had been offering me. Had I really repeatedly pushed away the one good thing that had ever come into my life?

But no, pushing him away was the right thing to do. Because look where his honor and steadfastness got him–tied to a felony burglary. An accomplice to a major crime.

Hayes was better off without me. He'd hurt, but

he'd recover. He'd find someone else to love. That's the kind of man he was.

And that's when the tears finally fell. Thinking about Hayes moving on. Hating me and loving someone else. I covered my mouth to block the sob that erupted from my throat.

Oh God.

How would I ever make it through this? My heart would never know how to beat again.

———

HAYES

I DIDN'T GO BACK to the house. Not right away. I couldn't be around people. Instead, I got into my truck and drove.

Fuck, I had been played. I was so damn stupid. So love sick that I'd actually committed a felony last night for a woman who was a criminal.

A fucking criminal!

Had I wanted to believe her innocence so badly that I ignored all the evidence? Concocted a story that made her out to be a pawn where she was really the villain? Was I blinded because she was so beautiful?

She'd used me. Flat out used me.

Except...that wasn't fair. She'd tried to keep me away. Many times. I was the one who pushed myself onto her. And she'd been clear about using me—for sex. Which I had willingly offered.

Even criminals had sexual needs.

No, making her out as the bad guy didn't quite sit right, either.

But facts were facts. She'd been involved with Burns and her dad the whole time. Fuck, had the story she'd told me about her dad being held hostage been something she concocted to keep me from turning her in? Of course, it had. She'd even played on my heartstrings.

I had to accept the fact that I had terrible instincts when it came to women. Not only had I picked one who didn't want me, but I'd picked a criminal.

Fuck. I slammed my fist into the steering wheel then turned the truck and pointed it toward the compound. I should just let this go. Let her go. But I wanted to see that video feed of Megan on her porch. Maybe I was a sucker for more pain, but I needed to see it with my own eyes. To watch the proof that I'd been fucking played.

When I got back, I found Kennedy in the command room.

"Show me," I grunted.

He played the clip of Megan on her porch. When it finished, I said, "Play it again." I watched it six more times. Memorized the brief glance she sent the camera as she spoke. Tried to reconcile this conversation with the woman I thought I'd known.

Tried to Figure out how I'd been so duped. Oh yeah, by sass and a gorgeous body.

"There's something else," Kennedy said.

"What?"

"This." He scrolled back in the stored feed and hit play. It was the video of me leaving the house this morning.

"What is this?"

"Just keep watching." He fast forwarded, then set it to play.

I watched as Burns, his two goons, and a third man—Megan's father, by the looks of it—went into the house.

"Huh."

"I know, right?" Kennedy asked. "If these guys are

here...less than an hour before the call she made, then who was she talking to on the phone?"

"I dunno. The fence? If she's in on it with the other three, she might be the ringleader of this group."

A tight fist closed in my solar plexus.

"You think Megan's the one in charge of Burns? I told you his rap sheet was a mile long." Kennedy minimized the screen and turned and looked over his shoulder at me. "If she is, I'm really fucking impressed. What are you going to do?"

I scrubbed a hand across my face. Would I turn her in? It would mean turning myself in at the same time, which I was willing to do. I'd done the crime, I would take responsibility for it.

But the thought of Megan going to prison made me sick. She hadn't hurt anyone, only stolen an ancient knife. Straight wasn't going to go hungry because of what she did. Maybe he'd get better fucking security.

"Nothing. I'm going do what she's been asking me to do from the start," I said. "I'm gonna let her go."

———

MEGAN

AFTER A FEW HOURS OF DRIVING, I pulled off the highway and into Spokane. I had some cash, enough to check into a motel. I needed to lie low while I figured out what I was going to do.

I sat on the motel bed, hollow. I should take a shower. Or eat. Or brush my teeth.

But I couldn't do any of those things. I couldn't seem to even move from the edge of the bed. Lost.

I looked at my phone. My dad had texted, asking where I was.

There were messages from Hayes from earlier in the day, but then they stopped. He must've figured out I was gone.

He'd finally let me go.

I waited for more tears to come, but they didn't. I'd cried myself dry.

I scrubbed a hand over my face. It was time to stop wallowing in self pity and figure this situation out. I needed to take Burns down. My father, too. I didn't feel even a twinge of remorse for my thoughts.

My dad had used me. More than once. Even as a kid. I hadn't known better then, but I did now. And I'd fallen for it.

He didn't care about me. Not at all. I doubted he ever had. Had that been why my mother had left? She knew about his selfishness?

Burns probably had a buyer lined up for the blade. If I could somehow get the scoop on that and intercept it—notify the local authorities where and when it would be—I might be able to get myself free of this mess. Put Burns behind bars. He might throw me to the wolves at the same time, but over the last few hours, I'd decided it was worth the risk.

This wasn't the life I wanted for myself, and I'd rather be behind bars and disgraced than live as a criminal. As a patsy.

I called my dad's phone.

"Meggie. Where are you?"

"Spokane."

"So, you are coming." He sounded relieved. Jesus. He really was harboring some fantasy about the two of us joining forces for evil.

"Yes, I'm coming," I snapped. "I want my cut."

There was a pause on the line as my dad digested my new tone.

"Since apparently you and Burns were in on this together, I'm guessing you're getting a cut for getting me to do the job. And since I'm the one who did the job, I figure that cut belongs to me. All you did was get drunk and get beat up."

"Well...yeah, okay," he muttered. "Fair enough. I did the background work, but you pulled the job. We can split my share. Of course, hon."

I had to grind my teeth to keep from railing at my dad.

"Do you have the money?" I was fishing, but I couldn't be overt about it. My dad wasn't going to trust me with information about the business dealings. Not yet.

"No, but I'll have it tomorrow."

"Cash?"

I needed to know how the transaction would work–whether it was an electronic transfer, cash or crypto. Because he wasn't giving me anything until he had his cut.

"Yeah, cash."

That was good. That meant there would be a physical meeting.

"I'm coming to the meet. I want my share." I tried to sound greedy. It was the way my dad thought, so it should ring true to him.

"We'll discuss it when you get here."

I relaxed. That probably meant the meet was

happening in Spokane. There was still time to figure this out. Possibly fix it.

I frowned. Probably not, but I had to try.

I ended the call and looked at the phone. Realizing Hayes probably had the capability of tracking me if he wanted–not that I believed he'd want to–I dropped it on the floor and stomped on it until it broke. I'd buy a burner phone tomorrow.

It was time to leave everything about my old life behind. That meant Hayes, Sparks, and the happiness I'd found there.

————

HAYES

"SHE DID WHAT?" Mrs. L asked.

The pot roast had been in the crock pot all day. The last thing I wanted to do was sit down and eat it when I wanted to take an AR-15 out into the back forty and shoot up some shit. But one look from the woman, and I had my butt in one of the dining room chairs.

I'd been so grim she wanted to know what was wrong. "Don't tell me it's security business. No one else at this table looks like their puppy got kicked." She gave me a kind look.

So, I told her. It wasn't Alpha Mountain business, and it was far from classified.

I repeated myself. "She stole a Viking dagger from Lucas Straight." I took the bowl of mashed potatoes from Kennedy. He kept the spoon and dropped a huge dollop on my plate for me.

"The actor?" she asked.

"Yes, ma'am."

Mrs. L blinked as she held a bowl of peas. "You're telling me that Megan Hager, the deputy who looks like a beauty pageant contestant, stole from Lucas Straight?"

"Yes."

Ford took the bowl from Mrs. L and spooned some on his plate.

"How? It wouldn't be like her to ever use her looks for any kind of gain."

I frowned. "She climbed up the rock chimney, went through a skylight and broke into a glass case."

"While Straight and his wife were sleeping," Kennedy added.

I glanced at him, and he looked impressed, almost full of parental pride. I wanted to punch his face in.

"Megan Hager?" Mrs. L asked again.

"Gram, I've never seen you so surprised before," Ford commented.

"I... well, I guess I shouldn't be."

"Why's that?" Taft asked then shoved a piece of pot roast in his mouth. Nothing was messing with his appetite.

She sighed. "Her father was a con man. Things were stolen in town back in the day. Indi's parents' hardware store was burgled."

Ford frowned. Indi wasn't here to confirm what Mrs. L said, but none of us doubted her.

"One day, it all stopped. It was pretty clear to everyone in town that it wasn't any coincidence it matched with when the Hagers moved away."

Kennedy nudged my arm and glared at my plate. I speared a carrot and tried to eat, but I just couldn't.

"If Colin Hager was a thief, then it makes sense he taught Megan," Mrs. L said. "They were close."

"He did." I attempted another bite. I was furious, but I knew I needed to have some manners. "Megan told me they did jobs together in Seattle after they left here when she was a kid. Until the last one where she was caught, and he left her to do the time."

Mrs. L's eyes widened. "This is news to me."

Ford grunted. Clearly, this didn't happen very often.

"She went to juvie for a year," I added. "Then went on to the academy. Supposedly went straight."

"Supposedly? Are you saying that she's been a cat burglar on the side for the past... ten years? That she leads a double life? Megan?" Mrs. L's voice dripped with doubt. "I can't believe that. With her looks, she'd stand out. She's far from forgettable."

I had to agree with Mrs. L. I would never forget Megan. Not in a million years.

Still... "I'm going to try to forget her," I grumbled. The food settled like ash in my stomach. "I'm not sure if I can ever forgive her for this."

Mrs. L pushed her pot roast around on her plate. No one spoke, everyone else shoveling the dinner into their mouths. I sat and felt like shit.

"She doesn't seem like someone who's rolling in extra cash. She drives an old car. Her house is small. I really find it hard to believe," Mrs. L said again.

Taft shrugged. "I guess you never know about a person."

Mrs. L fixed him with a look. "Is that really true, though? I think I'm a pretty good judge of character. I'm not usually wrong about people. Megan's dad was a bad apple, but Megan?" She shook her head. "I don't see it."

I stared at my plate as something in my brain tried to come through. Something had been nagging at me since I'd watched that security feed.

"Fuck!" I threw my napkin down and stood up from the table so fast I caused it to lift and thud.

"Hey! Watch it," Ford growled.

"She knew we watched her feed," I said to Kennedy. "She knew it because I told her we'd seen Burns on it before." My heart thudded with the realization.

Kennedy stared at me blankly.

"She looked at the camera while she was talking on the phone."

"I don't follow."

"This is a person who orchestrated a high-tech heist. She would know when she was being watched by security cameras, especially if they were her own. *She wanted me to hear that.* She was making sure I wouldn't follow."

"That makes no sense," Quincy said. "She knows you'll eventually watch the security footage, so she intentionally lies? Why even do it?"

I grabbed my plate and went to the sink to scrape

off the uneaten food. "She *wants* me to think she's bad, so I'll stay out of it."

"Why?" Quincy tossed up her hands.

"She might think she's protecting me. When she stole the dagger, I asked her why she did it alone." I put my dish in the dishwasher and leaned against the edge. "She said she was protecting me because I'm too honorable to break the law."

"Oh." Mrs. L set her hand on her chest. "Now that sounds more like the Megan I know."

"So, you think she's making sure you hate her enough to stay away," Quincy said.

"Yes." I pointed at Kennedy. "I bet if you look at her call logs, there wasn't one at that time."

"She was faking," Kennedy said thoughtfully. "Yeah, could be."

"I need to find out. One way or another, I need to know the truth." I looked to Quincy. "I need a lift."

Our helicopter pilot stood from the table. "Where to, sailor?"

"Kennedy, can you get me a location?"

"Already on it." My brother-in-arms was up and moving toward the sewing room.

"Hayes, are you sure you're not grasping at straws here?" Ford asked, doubt creasing his face.

I scrubbed a hand over my face. "I might be," I

admitted. I'd been stupid when it came to Megan. I pointed in the direction of Mrs. L. "But you heard what your gram said. She believes Megan's a good person."

"Well, go find out," Ford said mildly.

"I've got a location," Kennedy hollered from command central. "She's in Spokane."

"Meet you at the helipad," Quincy said, already leaving through the front door.

CHAPTER
TWENTY-FIVE

MEGAN

I TOSSED AND TURNED, finding it impossible to get any sleep. I thought of my father's twisted plan. I thought of how it had worked. I'd fallen for it like the biggest dupe.

I thought about Burns and how I would never work for him. About Hayes and how I missed him in my bed.

But even with all that swirling around in my idiotic brain, I somehow fell asleep because I was jolted awake by the sound of the chain on the motel door slipping out of the lock. I scrabbled to reach for the gun beneath my pillow and sat up, aiming at the door.

"If you're going to shoot, do it now." That hard, raspy voice made me go still. "I'm fucking tired of having that gun pointed at me."

Hayes. He was here. A thrill of happiness shot right through me. I'd missed him, even if it had been less than a day. I could smell him, recognize him anywhere by that dark scent.

I set the gun on the bedside table and flew out of bed in his direction. I stopped short of throwing myself at him, though. He might be here to turn me in. To bring me to justice for my crimes. I blinked in the darkness, finding the edges of his tall, dark form.

"You found me," I whispered.

"Yeah." He gave nothing away in the rough sylla- ble. Not where his heart stood. Or his head.

My fingers tangled with each other, fighting to keep from touching him. "Are you here to turn me in?"

The air between us charged with electricity that only grew when he didn't answer me at first.

"Is that what you need from me?"

I blinked in the darkness. Okay. Weird question. But it gave me hope. Hayes was here to talk about *us*, not about what he thought I'd done.

"No," I whispered.

"What is it you need?" His voice was a low rumble. Not suggestive, but the anger I heard earlier was gone.

"You." I spoke without thinking. Honestly. I should still be lying, trying to keep him out of this, but I didn't have it in me anymore. I'd left my bludgeoned heart back in Sparks with him when I drove away, and I'd learned a few things about myself on that long drive.

That I didn't want to live without Hayes.

That he was a man worth fighting for, and I'd been nothing but a coward. That I'd thought I was protecting him, but I was killing us both in the process.

I heard Hayes' breath catch, but he didn't reach for me. He didn't reassure me or overpower me this time. He just stood there, leaving the last foot of distance between us.

"I was a fool to run." My voice broke. "Stupid to push you away and leave you behind. You're all that matters to me, Raf."

Hayes caught my nape and pulled me in, stopping before our bodies collided, still keeping those few inches of separation between our bodies. They felt like a mile.

I tilted my face up to his, felt his breath feather across my lips. "Yeah?" His voice was rough and wounded.

I'd hurt him.

I knew that. He may still even think the worst of me—that I was the criminal mastermind behind it all like I'd wanted him to believe.

Yet he was here, asking what I needed from him.

I told him everything. Finally, I opened my heart to him.

"My dad was working with Burns all along," I choked out. "It was a con to get me to do the job because he couldn't with his broken collarbone. They showed up at my house and recorded me saying I'd stolen the dagger to blackmail me into joining them."

My heart pounded as Hayes digested that without speaking. "And are you?"

"*No.* I'm going to try to find out where their meet is to sell the dagger and call in the FBI. I may go down with them, but at least I'll be finished with this."

"Alone." He said it like an accusation. An arrow he pulled out of his own heart and thrust back at me.

"I fucked up," I admitted. "I'm sorry, Raf. I should have come to you instead of running. I should have told you the truth. I was shaken by my dad's betrayal. I felt tainted, and I didn't want any of it to touch you. But I swear to you now that I'm done running. I'm done pushing you away. If you forgive me, if you take me back--" My voice broke. I drew in a steadying breath. "I will never push you away again. I'm all in, Rafael Rebel Reyes, if it's not too late. With you. With us."

Hayes lips slammed down on mine in a hard, bruising kiss. He grasped the back of my head to hold me firm as he slanted his lips over mine, swept his tongue into my mouth. The kiss went on for a moment, then he slowly eased back. "You'd better not ever leave again."

"I won't, I promise."

"That conversation you had on your stoop? Was it for my benefit?"

Of course, he'd figured it out. Hayes knew me too well and was too smart to be fooled by my misdirection. I nodded. "I'm sorry. I thought maybe I could make you hate me to keep you away. I wanted to protect you. But I hated myself for doing it, and as soon as I drove away, I knew I'd ruined the only good thing in my life. You're the best thing that's ever happened to me, and I tried to destroy it. I... I chose a father who doesn't give a shit about me instead of you, who actually wants me." A tear leaked from the corner of my eye and spilled over Hayes's thumb where he cradled my face.

"It's okay, baby doll," he said softly. "I'm here. You'll have to do worse than that to make me bail."

"Raf." I threw myself at him, straddling his waist, my arms wrapped around his neck like he was a buoy, and I was drowning in deep waves.

"I got you." His strong arms banded around my back, and he walked me toward the bed. He tried to lower me to it, but I wouldn't let go, pulling him down on top of me. He settled over me, his hips resting between my parted legs. I felt him, hard and thick, through his clothes and my panties and t-shirt.

"Do you think so poorly of my skills?" he asked.

I frowned up at him. The room was so dark I barely caught the gleam in his eye from the sliver of streetlight that came in through the part in the curtains.

"What?"

"I'm a trained Navy SEAL with a merc team behind me. You think I couldn't get myself out of anything Burns and your dad threw at me? At us?" He stroked my hair back from my face.

"That was before–"

"Before you found out your father wasn't really

in any danger and used you to steal a five-million-dollar knife?"

Tears spilled out of the corners of my eyes, but with him pinning me down, I couldn't wipe them away.

"Before Burns framed you into working for them? Before you stood outside and lied your ass off on a fake phone call, so I could think you were the bad guy?"

"Before I fully believed there was an *us,*" I replied. "Before I admitted to myself that I'm in love with you, and I have been from the start."

There. I said it.

Stripped bare.

Finally.

Those were the words that told him everything. That I'd been willing to *do* anything because of how I felt for him.

Hayes groaned as if something was ripped open inside of him. As if he was wounded without any cuts.

His mouth settled on mine. Hard. Anguish and relief filled. I opened for him instantly and his tongue found mine. We were lost, wild in just a kiss. I didn't know how long it went on for, but he finally lifted his head.

"You're getting punished for what you did." His voice sounded ragged.

I arched against him, rubbing over the bulge in his pants, loving the rough dominance he always brought to our lovemaking. Yes, I was finally calling it lovemaking and not sex. What we had was so far beyond sex.

"You liked your spanking too much last night for it to be effective. Maybe an ass fucking would get the point across."

"You want to fuck my ass to tell me you love me?" I asked, laughter bouncing in my chest, opening up all the spaces that had caved in over the past twelve hours.

A slow grin spread across his face. "I've been showing it every fucking day since I met you, baby doll. I can tell that you like the idea."

"That you love me?"

"That, too. I meant me getting inside of that tight ass of yours. Sinking deep and giving both of us what we need."

I squirmed beneath him because I *really* liked the idea.

"Yeah, I can see that's not going to be a punishment either."

I worked the buckle on his belt, pulling it open and off. "Let's find out."

His chuckle was dark. "You *are* all in, aren't you?" He lowered his head and sank his teeth into the side of my breast through my t-shirt.

I moaned at the mingle of pain and pleasure.

"But then, you always have been with sex, haven't you, baby doll?"

"I'm all in with you, Raf." My hands were frantic to get the button open on his jeans. "And I'm pretty desperate to get you all in *me*."

"Oh, you're going to take me, baby doll. You're going to take me deep and hard, right in that tight little ass of yours." He turned me over and yanked down my panties, laying a flurry of spanks on my butt.

I welcomed the sting. I would welcome anything Hayes gave to me right now, my relief at fixing what I'd broken between us so complete.

"Beautiful woman," Hayes murmured, running his rough palm in a circle over my ass.

For once, the praise didn't irritate me. Because I wanted to be beautiful to Hayes. He made the ugliest parts of me–what was on the inside–come out clean. I arched my back, pushing my ass out for him, eager for all he had to give.

"I have lube in my suitcase," I told him.

He climbed off me and flipped on the bathroom light, stalked to the dresser where I'd opened the suitcase. "You packed a vibrator?" He sounded offended.

"I thought we were breaking up." I pulled my t-shirt over my head and tossed it to the floor, then wriggled out of the panties wrapped around my thighs.

A heavy thud indicated he'd tossed my vibrator in the trash. "You won't be needing that, baby doll. When you have needs, *I'll* be satisfying them."

I smiled. "You always do."

"On second thought." Hayes went back and grabbed the vibrator out of the trash, then took it to the bathroom to wash. "I might have use for this tonight."

I sat on the edge of the bed and waited. Hayes was in charge, and for once, I was going to follow his lead.

"Touch that pussy, get her nice and wet for me," Hayes instructed from the bathroom.

I spread my knees and slid my fingers between my legs. I was already damp in anticipation of what-ever Hayes had planned, but the moment my fingers started to move through my folds, slickness coated my flesh. I rubbed a slow circle around my clit, watching Hayes as he came toward me with dark purpose shining in his gaze.

"Good girl." He took my elbow and tugged me up from the bed. "Turn around and bend over."

I obeyed, and he tucked the buzzing vibrator lengthwise over my pussy, not inside me, but where I could grind down on it. "Let's see how you did." He stroked his fingers over my wet pleats. "Mmm. Nice and juicy, aren't you?"

"Mmm hmm."

He nudged my feet wider. "Your job is to work that sweet pussy of yours. Use that vibrator to keep yourself nice and wet here, understand?" He delivered a slap to my pussy.

"Yes!"

"Good girl." He rubbed over my entrance again then used the moisture he found there to circle my anus.

I puckered up at the foreign yet not unpleasant sensation.

He smacked my ass. "Uh uh." He delivered several more spanks. "You're getting your ass fucked, baby doll. Now open up." He squeezed a dollop of lube at my back entrance and used it to work his finger inside me.

I ground down on the vibrator, concentrating to stay relaxed and open for him, despite the urge to tighten around his finger.

"That's it, sweetheart." He reached another digit down to my pussy. "Are you still nice and wet for me?"

"God, yes," I moaned. Having my ass penetrated at the same time my clit was in contact with the vibrator was an overload of sensations. We'd only just begun, and I was already close to the finish line.

Hayes let out a soft curse and eased his finger out. I heard his zipper drop and the rustle of his jeans hitting the floor as he toed off his boots. A moment later, he pushed his cock into my sopping channel.

I moaned with satisfaction. Being filled with him felt like a completion. The destination I'd been seeking. But it was short-lived. He only gave me a few long strokes before he pulled out and rubbed lube on his cockhead, then applied more to my back hole.

I grunted, instinctively tightening, then forcing my muscles to relax. I exhaled a measured breath.

"Good girl. You want to take a good pounding in the ass, don't you, baby doll?"

God help me, I so did.

He slapped my ass. "Don't you?"

"Yes," I breathed. The stretch was intense as he applied steady pressure, easing in. Once his cockhead passed through, I groaned.

He stilled then, began to push on. It got easier, taking him. I both loved and hated the sensation at the same time. It was beyond intimate. The feeling of erotic fullness was like nothing I'd experienced before. My legs shook as I struggled to stay relaxed, to not tense around him, because when I did, the stretching sensation was worse.

I whimper-moaned, again and again, louder and louder, as he built a slow and steady pace, thrusting smoothly in and out, blowing my mind with each claiming thrust. The motion pushed me onto the vibrator that I held between my legs.

"Please," I started to beg. I didn't know whether I wanted him to finish, or I needed to come. Both, I guessed.

"Are you okay, baby doll?" Hayes pushed my hair back from my face to look at me.

"Yeah," I panted. "It's good. Please..."

"You need to come?"

"I...yes...please."

Hayes gripped my shoulder, his fingers tightening with his own need as he picked up speed.

"Oh God..." It was too much and also just

perfect. It was mind-shattering. Life-altering. A punishment and fulfillment in one.

I'd never needed to come so badly in my life.

I'd never trusted anyone with my body this way. Submitted like this. Surrendered to love.

"Raf...Raf, please," I begged.

He stroked in and stayed there, holding our hips together. "Put that vibrator inside, baby doll."

"Oh," I gasped. I tried to shift, but my mind was so far gone, I could hardly figure out what to do. Hayes pulled my hips away from the bed and helped feed the vibrating cylinder inside me until the curved head bumped up against my G-spot.

I squealed at the sensation.

"That's right. I'm gonna have you screaming by the time I'm through with you."

"Yes, ohmygod, yes!" I moaned. "Oh, please." I was babbling. Out of my mind already.

Hayes started pumping in and out of my ass, while the steady hum of the vibrator filled my pussy, making my entire pelvis buzz.

I moaned and whimpered, rubbed my face in the bedsheets, wrapped my fingers in them and tugged.

"You're taking it like a good girl, aren't you, baby doll? You like having your ass fucked hard by me?"

"Yes," I cried.

"This is your punishment, sweetheart." He wrapped his fist around my hair and tugged back. "This is what you get when you run from me."

"Oh, *gawd* yes!" I shrieked. I couldn't take much more. Like not another second. "Raf! Hayes!" The desperation rang out in my voice.

"Who fucks you hard when you're bad, baby doll?"

"*Ohmygod, you! You do!*" I probably woke the entire motel. Hayes wanted me... screaming? Mission accomplished. I guessed a Navy SEAL never backed down from a challenge.

"Fuck, yeah." Hayes thrust even harder, making me gasp and cry out, downright insane with need. "I'm going to come in your ass, and you're going to take it. You ready?"

"Yes! Oh please."

The bed bounced with Hayes' thrusts, but he kept them smooth, not growing erratic, which would hurt.

"Now, baby doll." Hayes thrust deep and shouted.

I was working so hard to stay relaxed for him and couldn't seem to come. Not until he reached back and pumped the vibrator in and out of my pussy, his cock still stuffed in my ass.

Then I screamed and came, my muscles contracting around his dick and the vibe as I sobbed out my release in the sheets. I collapsed, wilted, replete. Sated.

"Aw, fuck, baby doll. That was so good." Hayes stroked my hair back from my face, kissed along my jaw. "Are you okay? Was I too rough?"

"I'm okay." My voice sounded far away. I was blissed out beyond description. Spun out into the atmosphere like a satellite orbiting the Earth.

"You sure?" He bit my earlobe.

"Mmm hmm."

Slowly, carefully, he eased out of me then removed the vibrator. "Stay right there, baby doll." He went to the bathroom to wash up, returning with a cloth for me. He cleaned me then laid a tender kiss on my shoulder blade. "Good girl."

"Am I?" I asked sleepily. I was so blissed out, my limbs felt like rubber.

"Mmm hmm. *My* good girl."

"Yep, definitely yours," I muttered.

CHAPTER TWENTY-SIX

HAYES

I HELPED Megan fully onto the bed and crawled in beside her, pulling the sheets up and around us with a snap.

"Raf?" she murmured.

"Yeah?"

"How'd you find me? And how'd you get here so fast?" She rolled over to face me.

I took her into my arms, loving the way she nestled into my chest. This was the woman who refused to cuddle. Who wanted me out of her bed and her house as soon as we'd both come.

I stroked her silky hair. "Kennedy tracked your

phone, and Quincy flew me in the helicopter."

"Wow. You guys really are a formidable team, aren't you?"

"Yeah. We've dealt with insurgents and terrorists. Don't be afraid of Burns or your dad. My team can handle them before breakfast."

She ran her nails through my chest hair, lightly scratching me in a way that was about pleasure without being sexual.

I caught one of her hands and brought it to my lips to kiss. "I love you, Megan." I hadn't said it yet, and it felt important.

"I know." She leaned in and pressed a kiss to my chest, then my neck, then my chin. "You don't have to tell me. Your actions show it. You've never wavered. Never left me. Even when I kept leaving you day after day."

"I'm never going to leave you," I vowed. She should know it by now, but with her past, I probably couldn't say it enough.

"I know. I do." She held my jaw and kissed me with an open mouth. Our tongues tangled. Breath mixed. Then she settled her head on my shoulder, right where I wanted it for the rest of my life.

"So, what was your plan, here?" I asked after a moment of silence. "I'm guessing you had one."

She drew a breath and sighed. "It's not great. I was going to try to get my dad to divulge the buyer or the meeting location for when Burns sells the dagger. It hasn't happened yet, I know that much. He said tomorrow, or...what time is it? I guess, today. The trouble is, my dad's smart, and he's suspicious, as a con man should be. I haven't figured out how to get him to spill."

I stroked my fingertips up and down her bare spine. "Can you get him to take you along? If so, you don't have to know ahead of time. We can wire you and then follow the men to the meet."

It would be easy as fuck.

"And then what? What are you going to do with them?" she asked. "I mean, you can't kill them."

I laughed, and she shifted on my chest. "You've been watching too many movies. They'll be arrested."

"By whom? It can't be me. Not only do I not have jurisdiction, but I stole the dagger. We'll have to call in the Feds."

"That's what I was thinking, too. Burns is slippery when it comes to convictions. This would be an easy one. Caught with the stolen item, with the buyer."

"And my dad?" she asked.

"Him, too. You okay with that?" She'd committed grand larceny because she cared enough for the guy. I had to wonder if she'd be okay about this.

"Putting him in jail? Yes. Hopefully for a long time," she muttered.

I kissed the top of her head.

"We can even hand the buyer over to the Feds. They'll be sending us gift cards to Applebee's for all we did for them."

She laughed.

"Sounds good. I'll go to the meet, and your team will follow."

"If you don't want to go, we'll think of another way."

"I stole the dagger. I want to see this through."

I couldn't blame her.

"Especially since I'm going to jail, too. We should just make it easy for them."

I shifted, so I was on my side looming over her. "You're not going to jail."

She brought her hand up and cupped my jaw. "I'm a law enforcement officer who broke the law. Burns has the proof."

"We can make people disappear. Permanently. You think Kennedy can't delete a little bit of digital evidence?"

"Hayes."

She thought she was headed to jail. No fucking way.

"I know of a way to keep you out. To make you the good guy."

She stared at me, clearly doubtful, but she whispered, "Okay. Tell me."

———

MEGAN

I WENT to the address Burns had texted. Hayes hated that I was going to see Burns on my own. I'd reassured Hayes I hadn't done the man any good dead, and Hayes hadn't responded well to that. Still, it was Hayes' plan, and I had to go in alone.

I climbed from my car thinking about the supposed job Burns had for me. I didn't care about it. There was no way in hell I was doing it or anything else for the guy. I was here for one reason and one reason only.

To put my dad and Burns behind bars and get my life back.

It was a shitty warehouse in a shitty part of town.

One of the goons who had been at my house manned the dented door. I gave him a chin lift as greeting, and he opened the door for me.

That was easy.

"Meg!" my dad called from across the space. From what I could guess, it had been a factory at some point decades ago. There was a rickety-looking conveyer belt high in the air along with other metal contraptions that I couldn't guess what they did. There was an office off to one side, but it didn't seem like anyone lived here. It was more of a stupid clubhouse or something.

I accepted my father's hug with a mental grimace. Seeing him only made me hate him more. I could see now with such vivid clarity that he'd used me my entire life. He was so selfish. I felt sick. I'd loved him, even after he left me high and dry. I hadn't forgiven him, but I'd still cared.

I had. I'd broken into the Straight's house the other day.

No more.

I knew what real love was like with Hayes. It wasn't tainted. There were no conditions tied to it. No deals or coercion. No lies.

"I'm here. I want to know about my cut."

Dad laughed. The bruising around his eyes was

fading. He looked happy, which made me want to throat punch him.

Stick to the plan!

"Greedy?"

I frowned. "I learned from the best."

He preened at the praise, missing the sarcasm. "Sure did. We're meeting the buyer today."

"I'm going."

"No."

We turned at the voice. Burns approached.

"Your loyalty hasn't been proven yet."

I crossed my arms. "I stole the dagger." I glanced around at the men who were part of his *gang*. There were about six of them of varying ages. "What did these men do? Huh? Nothing. I'm the one who brought you a five-million-dollar payoff."

Burns studied me.

"Why keep me away? You think I'm going to steal the dagger from you?" I laughed. "I stole it once, I can steal it again. It doesn't matter if I'm there or not."

"She has a point," my dad said, slapping me on the shoulder. "I taught her everything she knows."

I did everything in my power not to roll my eyes.

Burns frowned. "Fine. We leave in an hour."

CHAPTER
TWENTY-SEVEN

HAYES

WE HAD MORE eyes and ears on Megan than we had on the insurgent leaders in Afghanistan. Ford called his contact at the FBI, and they'd been more than interested in what we knew about the dagger. After Straight had contacted the authorities, the FBI themselves had gotten involved. To have an open and shut case and nab Burns in the process?

Their dicks were hard at the opportunity.

Yet I was the only one who had skin in this game. It was my woman who was in there with those assholes. It wasn't a Boy Scout pack meeting she'd dropped in on. They were dangerous thugs, and I didn't like her anywhere near them. I had a feeling she'd be the only one in the place without a weapon.

But she dealt with the wrong side of the law at work, so it wasn't as if she was a soccer mom not up for the challenge. Megan Hager would do this and do it fucking well. I was proud of her. I wanted to hug her and fuck her and wrap her in bubble wrap.

"She's doing just fine," Kennedy said.

We were in my truck a block away. One of the things Alpha Mountain didn't have was a fancy van like on TV shows. We didn't do surveillance, at least not at this low level. And usually not in the US. Kennedy had his powerful computer opened on his lap, and the speaker was turned up, so we could hear everything around Megan.

Her dad was there. Burns was there. The meet was going to happen soon.

"Everyone's on standby," Kennedy said.

I knew this. All of it. I wasn't an idiot, and he wasn't being patronizing.

But I was squeezing the steering wheel in a stranglehold, so he couldn't miss my tension. And worry.

"Yeah," I muttered.

"I'm going to find a woman who's a preschool teacher," Taft said. "So, the only exciting thing she has going on in her life is that she likes to bake cookies and play with puppies."

That had me laughing and looking at my friend. "Sounds boring as fuck."

"Sure does, but at least she won't be in the center of danger every fucking day."

I frowned.

"Ready, Meg? It's like old times, isn't it? You and me? Robbing the world?" Colin Hager laughed.

I growled. "I hate that fucker."

———

MEGAN

I KNEW THE PLAN. Knew Hayes was out there. So was the FBI, and they didn't take too kindly to fellow law enforcement officers going to the Dark Side. They threw the book at bad cops.

That was me. The bad cop.

In the room was Burns with the evidence that I'd stolen the dagger. The dagger itself. A buyer for the dagger. Money in exchange for the stolen goods. It was an open and shut scenario where I ended up doing five to ten in federal prison.

I would be punished, and it wasn't the good kind Hayes doled out. There was no pleasure in what could happen to me.

But I trusted Hayes. I did. I loved him and believed him when he said he had a plan. And a team for support.

So, I walked into a meet in the penthouse suite of a Spokane hotel with a wire and a fuck-ton of faith.

The buyer–I'd yet to learn his name–turned out to be a guy in his sixties with two goons who could be related to Burns' based on looks and demeanor. He was upbeat, completely relaxed and practically drooling for the stupid dagger.

It was me, my father and Burns. His hooligan duo waited outside in the hall.

Burns pulled the dagger from the inner pocket of his coat. "Money, please."

The buyer nodded, and one of his men went to the bedroom and returned with a briefcase. He set it on the dining table and opened it. My dad went to it and lifted a wrapped bundle.

The case was filled to the brim with cash, which I assumed totaled five million dollars.

"This the one who stole it?" The man looked to me.

"My daughter. Beautiful and talented," my father said, his words full of pride.

The man looked me over in a way I didn't like. I narrowed my eyes at him.

"I may have other jobs with your... skill set." He flicked his brows.

"She works for me. You want something to add to your collection, you let *me* know," Burns told him.

Great. Burns wanted to pimp me out. What an ass. As a woman, I hated that he'd have to get his cut on something I did all the hard work for.

"You have an interest in all things Viking?" I asked.

My father closed the lid on the briefcase and took it. Burns handed over the dagger, and the buyer held it and studied it as if it were a precious infant, not hundreds of years old.

"It is the central piece to my collection. I missed the auction for it, and Lucas Straight refused to sell. My ancestors were Viking, and I wish to believe this belonged to one of them."

"Well, that doesn't mean it belongs to you," I said full of snark.

With that, all hell broke loose.

The door was kicked in.

"FBI! Hands up!"

A swarm of people with FBI emblazoned on their shirts or jackets stormed the suite.

The buyer's men reached for weapons beneath their jackets and were immediately subdued.

I raised my hands over my head as I stepped back and watched it all unfold. No one touched me.

Burns was patted down and handcuffed. My dad, the same. It took less than thirty seconds, and it was over.

"What about her?" Burns shouted, wiggling like a snagged fish in an agent's hold when he noticed I wasn't being cuffed.

"I'm with them," I said.

"What the fuck, Meg?" my father asked.

"She stole the dagger," Burns said, pushing the blame to me.

"I'll make a deal. Her for information," my father offered, desperately looking to the agent beside him.

Unbelievable. I dropped my hands and stared at him. Any bit of feeling I had for the man was gone. Crushed beneath his cruel words. He was going to give me up for his freedom. Just like he had on the job when I was seventeen.

"That your daughter?" the agent asked him.

"We worked together. She was caught with the

Empress ring, but I know other jobs she did. Unsolved crimes."

The agent shook his head. "You'd throw your own daughter under the bus? What an asshole."

"In my phone," Burns said. "The proof she stole the dagger. Arrest me for fencing stolen goods, but that's all that's happening here." Technically, what Burns said was true, and that meant he'd do less time, if any, if he had a good lawyer.

"What proof?" Hayes came in the room. Kennedy was right behind him.

God, he looked so good. Larger than life. And all mine. Feel-good endorphins flooded my system just at the sight of him. It was almost like a post-orgasmic high.

"I didn't find any proof on your phone, Burns," Kennedy told him.

"Who the fuck are you?" he snapped.

"He's irrelevant." Hayes glared at Burns. "I'm the one you should remember because you fucked with the wrong woman. *My* woman." He looked to me. "You okay, baby doll?"

I nodded. I wasn't in the clear yet. I wouldn't do any time because I helped bring Burns and the buyer to justice. My dad was small time, but he'd go down, too, which was fine with me. Still, I'd be known as a criminal. I'd have no job. My career was over.

"Ms. Hager. I wanted to introduce myself." In strode Lucas Straight and Ford.

I blinked. So did Burns and my father.

"Lucas Straight." The actor offered his hand to me to shake. "I want to thank you for your effort in testing my security."

I blinked again while he turned to one of the FBI men. Hayes hadn't told me any of this. "Alpha Mountain Security did a great job with my vacation home. I am humbled and shamefaced to admit that what I thought was a good alarm system was a total failure. That's not speaking poorly of Ms. Hager. In fact, it was top of the line, and she got past it."

"What the fuck?" Burns said.

Ford set his hand on Lucas Straight's shoulder. "That's why you pay us the big bucks. We only hire the best consultants. With a background like Megan's, she's the only one for the job. When I heard she'd learned from the best–isn't that what you said, Hager?" He glanced at my father, but only briefly, as if he wasn't worth his energy. "Nabbing the Empress ring at seventeen. Such talent. Since she did the crime for her involvement, she did her time. Years in law enforcement show her true colors. Her honor."

"What better person to test my system than a thief?" Lucas Straight looked pleased. He was an even better actor than I knew. "And to know I helped in bringing down some bad guys. It's like out of a movie..." He winked at me as he shook Ford's hand again and left the suite.

Holy shit. Straight saved me in the best and most obvious way possible. He made me out to be a thief, just as I had been. But one with a purpose. For good. And while they might discover I'd done the Empress job, I'd completed my sentence. That job held no sway any longer.

I looked to Hayes, who curled a finger, beckoning me over.

I went to him but stopped in front of my dad first. Looked him in the eye. Then punched him in the gut.

He bent at the waist, the FBI agent behind him holding him up by the cuffs at his low back.

"Fuck, Meg."

"Did you feel it that time?" I asked then walked off into Hayes' arms.

And my future.

CHAPTER
TWENTY-EIGHT

HAYES

"THANK YOU FOR THE LIFT, QUINCY." I thumped our pilot on the back as we walked off the helipad back at Ford's property that night. I had to admit, while the helicopter was a hefty expense for the company, to me, it was worth every fucking penny.

It had been just over twenty-four hours since she'd flown me to Spokane to go after Megan. Everything had changed since then. Not just with Megan's situation but with us. For the first time, I felt like she was actually *with* me. Not sharing a little fun in bed or only a piece of herself.

She'd held my hand on the flight home, sending me small smiles.

Now, she looked weary but more relaxed than I'd ever seen her. With all the details of her life, it all made sense. Her need to remain aloof, her job as a deputy, the fact that she was alone and had wanted to stay that way. Her need for closeness without the danger of intimacy.

"Megan, my gram is making sandwiches with the leftover pot roast from last night. Some of us ducked out early. Why don't you join us for dinner?" Ford suggested. I had no doubt he'd called her with an update. She was involved in our relationship as much as anyone else. And, she was a knowing sort and being left out probably drove her crazy.

Part of me wanted to hustle Megan off to be alone with her, but dinner with the team felt right. They'd just stuck their necks out for her, and we both owed them the camaraderie and group celebration that came after a successful mission. My dick *was* hard like after every mission, but for a completely different reason now.

"That sounds nice, thanks," Megan agreed. Gone was the slightly standoffish demeanor she used to have when invited to do anything.

I took her hand, and she let me keep it as we walked together to the house.

"There they are!" Mrs. L stood on the front steps to welcome us in. She was in her usual jeans and casual top and the scent of meat and... home... wafted out the open doorway. I could understand why Ford returned here when he'd been kicked out of the Navy. It was his home and a comforting place, one I now considered home as well.

"I'm making sandwiches, did Ford tell you?" she asked.

"Yes, ma'am." I leaned in to kiss Mrs. L's cheek, standing two steps below hers, so we were the same height.

Her wise eyes flicked to Megan. "I see you brought our girl home. Everything go okay?"

"Yep," Ford answered, coming in behind us. "The FBI picked up Burns and Megan's dad. And the dagger buyer. Lucas Straight is not pressing any charges against Megan."

"Yeah, so how exactly did you manage that?" Megan spun to face Ford. We hadn't talked about how it had all worked out. I was surprised she took this long to ask.

He shrugged, gave her his usual intense gaze. "I just explained that you'd been blackmailed into stealing it and wanted to do the right thing and return it *and* bust the guys who'd forced you to do it at the same time. I asked if he'd be willing to say you'd done it as a test to his security. He's an actor who loves a good story. He said as long as he got the dagger back, he'd be happy to play along, and he wouldn't press charges, especially since you actually had proven his security was crap. He said he won't lie under oath, though, so if it goes to court, all bets are off."

"If it goes to court, I will tell the truth," Megan said.

"It won't." I wrapped my arm around her waist and led her to the kitchen where Quincy and Taft had already arrived. They were setting the table, no doubt put to work by Mrs. L.

Ford came in behind us and beelined straight for Indigo, who stood at the counter, slicing watermelon. She offered him a sly smile as he wrapped his arm around her waist and nuzzled into her neck as a greeting. He whispered something to her, but I couldn't hear.

"Sit while the food's hot," Mrs. L ordered.

We did as ordered. Mrs. L had set out the fixings for sandwiches along with corn on the cob and a Greek salad. There was plenty, as usual.

"Testing security systems as a private consultant would pay a lot more than the salary you make as a deputy," Ford observed.

"Hmm," Megan said noncommittally, grabbing a piece of corn from the platter.

"Lucas Straight hired us to install a system that will actually keep you out."

He paused, and then everyone started to laugh.

"The commission's yours, Megan," he said with a smile. "You more than earned it."

Her mouth dropped open.

"Oh... um, wow."

"I'd like to add it to the Alpha Mountain Security menu, if you're willing," he said. "Straight didn't blink at the quote for the install and for your retest. You up for scaling his chimney again?"

Megan blinked. "Really?"

"About the job and about breaking into his house? Yes."

It was actually a smart addition to the business model, and I had no doubt Straight would tell all his rich and fancy friends. That meant more business than ever.

"It could be full-time or a side job if you don't want to leave the Sheriff's Department."

She nodded thoughtfully, picking up her knife to

butter her corn. "Side job sounds fun. I'd like that, Ford. Thanks."

"Mrs. L, this looks amazing," I gushed, trying to make up for not eating last night. "And I am starving." I dropped four slices of homemade bread on my plate and two on Megan's. "Is that enough?"

"It's plenty." She reached past me to grab the platter of meat. The gestures were so simple–putting food on each other's plates–but what they symbolized to me was everything. We were acting like a couple. We *were* a couple. With family.

Megan had given herself to me. I no longer needed to chase her, to prove my faithfulness to her. She trusted. She believed in us. We were together now. Over corn and leftovers.

When we'd all assembled our sandwiches and stacked our plates, I lifted my beer. "Here's to another successful mission."

"Hooyah," Kennedy said, lifting his.

"Yeah, I want to say thank you to all of you. You really stuck your necks out for me, and I'm not really sure what I ever did to deserve that." Megan's voice broke a little.

"Oh phooey, you've done plenty to deserve it," Mrs. L scolded. "You're a good person, Megan Hager.

It doesn't matter who your dad is or how you were raised. I know character."

"It's true," I murmured, leaning in to kiss her temple. "Mrs. L is the one who never believed you were in on the deal with your dad. She made me think it through."

Megan blinked past a sheen of tears in her eyes.

"To our new teammate." Taft, who sat on her other side, clinked his beer bottle against Megan's.

"I'll drink to that." Quincy lifted her beer. "Glad to have another woman on the team." She took a sip. "Although you have Hayes attached to your hip, so we can't go out trolling for men together."

"Oh, I'll still be your wingwoman," Megan told her. "I didn't know that was something you needed."

Quincy shrugged and picked up her sandwich. "Well, yeah. I'm new to town. I need to get out there and circulate."

Kennedy frowned. "There's nowhere to circulate in Sparks," he snapped.

Was it me, or had he said it too quickly, like the idea of Quincy trolling for men pissed him off?

"Well, let's go out," Megan offered brightly, missing Kennedy's piss-off. "We can have a ladies' night. What's your type? Cowboy? Businessman? Law enforcement?"

Quincy blushed a little. "I was thinking more, uh, hot mechanic." She flushed some more.

Indi choked on her beer, and Megan laughed. "Lee Landers? Yeah, he's hot," Megan agreed.

"Who's *Lee Landers*?" Kennedy demanded. "He sounds like a porn star."

"Yeah, who are we talking about here?" Taft asked.

"Porn star?" Indi said with a laugh. "He's no one, never mind." She winked at Quincy. "Girls' night. We'll talk later."

"Yep, later." Megan smiled.

Mrs. L chuckled. "I guess I'm a little old for girls' night, aren't I?"

"Nah, you can come, too." Quincy beckoned.

"You helped with me and Megan. I'm sure you can help with Quincy," I told her.

Megan frowned, and Mrs. L gave me a wink.

"Hey, when is this girls' night?" Why was I already jealous of my woman's time? We'd only been an official couple for approximately twelve hours.

Megan picked up on it and reached for my hand. "Not tonight. I'm with you tonight, sailor."

"Ahh," Quincy said.

"Well, thanks for dinner, Mrs. L." I popped up

from the table. Sounded like Megan needed my services, and I was happy to oblige, as always.

"Young man, sit down and eat your food. Then you may take Megan off to canoodle."

I blushed at Mrs. L's order. Neither of us had eaten a bite, and it was the second night I wanted Megan over pot roast.

Everyone laughed as the two of us started eating. The conversation quieted as we all dug in.

I ate twice as fast as Megan, and once she was done, I grabbed her plate, took both our plates to the dishwasher and took her hand. We left the kitchen with a wake of laughter.

"Your place or mine?" I asked once we were far enough away from everybody, even though it was a no-brainer since my place was a bunkhouse.

"This way." Megan shifted our trajectory, pulling me down toward the barn. The sky had been clear all day, but clouds were settling over the mountains. It would probably rain overnight.

I laughed. "Don't tell me Megan Hager is sentimental."

"I might be." The smoldering look she tossed over her shoulder at me made my cock leap against my zipper.

"Is this our special place?" I pressed her up

against the barn wall–the one where I'd first made her come. Had it been only about a week ago? So much had happened since then.

"Uh huh." She untucked my shirt and slid her greedy hands up my torso.

I palmed her ass, squeezing and kneading it as I lowered my head to kiss her jaw. The chemistry was the same. The need intense. Fuck, I loved this woman.

"How do you want it, baby doll?"

She lifted her lips to meet mine, looping her arms around my neck as she kissed me. "However you want to give it." Her voice was pure honey.

"Aw, fuck, you're sweet." I lifted one of her knees to angle my thickened cock in the notch between her legs.

She rocked her hips to meet mine, and I ground against her, homing in on that delicious heat.

I unbuttoned her jeans and slid my hand inside her panties to curl my fingers into her. She was hot, wet and ready for me. "I seem to recall we did something like this last time."

Her head fell back on a groan, and her soft flesh squeezed.

I found her clit and circled it, roughly. "Was this what you were thinking?"

"Mmm hmm." She worked the button to my jeans open and returned the favor, sliding her hands inside my jeans to squeeze my cock. A gift of pre-cum seeped from the tip.

"You gonna run off without giving me your number when we're through?" I screwed one finger inside her.

"Uh uh." She shook her head, making her thick hair swish over her shoulders. Her eyes were glazed with lust. "Hayes."

"Raf," I reminded. I thrusted my finger in and out. "No, you're not, are you? Because you know I can give it to you good, don't you, Megan?"

"God, yes." She rolled my balls, then worked my shaft out of my boxer briefs.

"I'm going to give it to you good right now, baby doll. Then I'm going to give it to you even better back at your place. How's that sound?" I withdrew my finger and turned her around to face the barn wall, tugging her hips backward. I licked her sticky sweetness from my fingers which only made me harder.

She shimmied her jeans and panties down to give me access. "That sounds good."

"I'm gonna need a key, though. I'm done with breaking and entering." I rolled a condom on my straining dick then lined it up with her entrance.

"Do you want to move in?" she asked.

I went still, the head of my dick just tucked inside her snug channel. "Yeah." The syllable burst out of me like an exclamation, and I thrust deep inside her at the same time.

Hell, yeah, I wanted to move in. I wanted everything Megan had to offer. I wanted to be with her, soak up her essence, bask in the light of her beauty. Admire her strength, skill and prowess.

"Raf!"

I snapped my hips in and out, bracing her hips with an arm around her waist. "Is this what you needed, baby doll?"

"Definitely, yes. Soooo yes," she groaned, and I laughed.

"That's good, baby doll. I nipped at her ear as I continued to thrust. "Because all I want to do is make you scream."

"It's working," she choked.

"Good." I pounded harder, closing my eyes and savoring the moment—how good it felt to be inside her. The fact that she'd asked me to live with her. That she was truly and wholly mine now.

My thighs started to quake. My balls drew up tight. I used the pad of my middle finger to gently rub over Megan's clit. "Scream my name. Who makes you come?"

"Raf!" she gasped again. "Raf..." She let out a cry that sounded like she was working her way up to an honest-to-goodness scream, so I covered her mouth before it erupted.

I shoved in deep and tight to empty my balls a second before she shrieked around my fingers, and we came together, her tight cunt squeezing and milking the cum out of my dick. I shuddered out my release, holding Megan tightly and burying my face against her neck.

Her laugh was husky and sweet as I caught my breath. I eased out, and she turned around in my arms. "I love you, Raf."

"I love you, too, baby doll. So much."

"Come on," she said after I'd removed the condom and we'd both buttoned up. "Let's go home."

Home. I sure liked the sound of that.

EPILOGUE

HAYES

"SO I FINALLY GET A DATE WITH you." I held Megan's hand as we walked into the bowling alley. "It only took how many orgasms before you agreed to it?"

"I guess it's a little backward, isn't it?" Megan asked as we stood at the high counter. The sounds of pins being knocked down, the electronic sound of an arcade game and a crowded Saturday night surrounded us.

"What size?" the man questioned, setting my rental shoes before me.

"Eight," she replied.

"Maybe, but I'm enjoying wondering if you're going to let me kiss you on your front porch at the end of the night."

She rolled her eyes, but the smile that turned up the corners of her mouth was just what I was hoping for.

"Go pick out your ball, and I'll grab your shoes."

She nodded and went to the tiered rack to select the perfect weight from the options.

I snagged her rental shoes from the man and met her gaze. I pointed to lane twelve and headed that way. As I slid the velcro in place on my bowling shoes–yup, velcro–she set her ball in the ball return area. I went to the score computer and entered my name, Raf, and hers, BD.

"BD?" she asked, looking confused at the display up by the ceiling.

I grinned, then closed the few feet between us, leaned down and kissed her.

"Couldn't wait until later."

Her eyes went soft, and she was still smiling. Seeing her happy made my fucking day. It used to be that we took out a group of insurgents, or some missionaries were safely rescued. Now, my woman was content being with me in a bowling alley.

"BD?" she asked again.

"Baby doll."

I turned and grabbed a ball from the rack, felt its heft, then stepped up onto the lane. Raising the ball, I eyed the ten pins and took the steps and swung. The hefty ball thumped on the lane and careened toward the pins, taking them all out.

I spun around, grinning. I raised a pointed finger to my mouth and blew on it, pretending it was a gun.

Megan, in her simple jeans and green long-sleeved top that was more than modest but didn't hide any of her curves, grabbed her ball and stepped past me to take her turn.

"Hey, Deputy!"

A faceless voice called for her, and Megan turned toward it, waved with her free hand, then focused back on her objective. Before she bowled, she turned and faced me.

"Want to make this game a little more interesting?" she asked.

I was about to sit down but got close to her instead. "What did you have in mind? Strip bowling?"

She laughed and looked around. Almost every lane was taken with weekend bowling leagues, teenagers and families with small kids.

"Winner decides what we do next," she said.

My dirty mind went to all kinds of possibilities involving me bossing Megan around in bed. Not the best thoughts for keeping my dick down in front of half the town.

"You're on."

"Don't you wonder if I'm good at this? I mean, when I win, I might pick getting ice cream at the Sweet Cow stand."

It was a stand only open in the summer and was always packed.

"Baby doll, you win, I win, you'll be licking something. Or I will, and you know I love all that cream."

She flushed and smacked my arm. "Your mind is filthy."

I grinned. "Take your turn, baby doll. I can't wait to see what happens next."

I wasn't talking about the round of bowling either. I didn't know what the future would bring, but it wouldn't be boring. Not with Megan.

I went and sat down in front of the computer to watch my woman step three times, swing and send her ball down the center of the lane. Just like a pro.

I figured. There was nothing this woman didn't do well. She was a top-notch deputy. A world-class cat burglar. A thief who stole my heart.

She could have it. It was always meant for her, and I never wanted it back.

Ready for more Alpha Mountain?
Continue with Warrior!
Get it now!

NOTE FROM VANESSA & RENEE

Guess what? We've got some bonus content for you with Megan and Hayes. Yup, there's more!

Click here to read!

WANT FREE RENEE ROSE BOOKS?

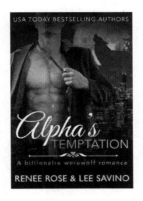

Go to http://subscribepage.com/alphastemp to sign up for Renee Rose's newsletter and receive a free copy of *Alpha's Temptation, Theirs to Protect, Owned by the Marine, Theirs to Punish, The Alpha's Punishment, Disobedience at the Dressmaker's* and *Her Billionaire Boss*. In addition to the free stories, you will also get special pricing, exclusive previews and news of new releases.

GET A FREE VANESSA VALE BOOK!

Join my mailing list to be the first to know of new releases, free books, special prices and other author giveaways.

http://freeromanceread.com

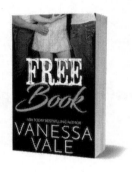

ALSO BY RENEE ROSE

Chicago Bratva

"Prelude" in Black Light: Roulette War

The Director

The Fixer

"Owned" in Black Light: Roulette Rematch

The Enforcer

The Soldier

The Hacker

Vegas Underground Mafia Romance

King of Diamonds

Mafia Daddy

Jack of Spades

Ace of Hearts

Joker's Wild

His Queen of Clubs

Dead Man's Hand

Wild Card

More Mafia Romance

Her Russian Master

Contemporary

Daddy Rules Series

Fire Daddy

Hollywood Daddy

Stepbrother Daddy

Master Me Series

Her Royal Master

Her Russian Master

Her Marine Master

Yes, Doctor

Double Doms Series

Theirs to Punish

Theirs to Protect

Holiday Feel-Good

Scoring with Santa

Saved

Wolf Ridge High Series

Alpha Bully

Alpha Knight

Bad Boy Alphas Series

Alpha's Temptation

Alpha's Danger

Alpha's Prize

Alpha's Challenge

Alpha's Obsession

Alpha's Desire

Alpha's War

Alpha's Mission

Alpha's Bane

Alpha's Secret

Alpha's Prey

Alpha's Sun

Shifter Ops

Alpha's Moon

Alpha's Vow

Alpha's Revenge

His Human Possession

Zandian Brides

Night of the Zandians

Bought by the Zandians

Mastered by the Zandians

Zandian Lights

Kept by the Zandian

Claimed by the Zandian

Stolen by the Zandian

Other Sci-Fi

The Hand of Vengeance

Her Alien Masters

Regency

The Darlington Incident

Humbled

The Reddington Scandal

The Westerfield Affair

Pleasing the Colonel

Western

ALSO BY VANESSA VALE

For the most up-to-date listing of my books:

vanessavalebooks.com

All Vanessa Vale titles are available at Apple, Google, Kobo, Barnes & Noble, Amazon and other retailers worldwide.

ABOUT RENEE ROSE

USA TODAY BESTSELLING AUTHOR RENEE ROSE loves a dominant, dirty-talking alpha hero! She's sold over a million copies of steamy romance with varying levels of kink. Her books have been featured in USA Today's *Happily Ever After* and *Popsugar*. Named Eroticon USA's Next Top Erotic Author in 2013, she has also won *Spunky and Sassy's* Favorite Sci-Fi and Anthology author, *The Romance Reviews* Best Historical Romance, and *has* hit the *USA Today* list eight times with her Bad Boy Alpha and Wolf Ranch series, as well as various anthologies.

Please follow her on Tiktok

Renee loves to connect with readers!
www.reneeroseromance.com
reneeroseauthor@gmail.com

ABOUT VANESSA VALE

A USA Today bestseller, Vanessa Vale writes tempting romance with unapologetic bad boys who don't just fall in love, they fall hard. Her 75+ books have sold over one million copies. She lives in the American West where she's always finding inspiration for her next story. While she's not as skilled at social media as her kids, she loves to interact with readers.